MOE "SNAKE EYES" JUAREZ
DETECTIVE STORIES

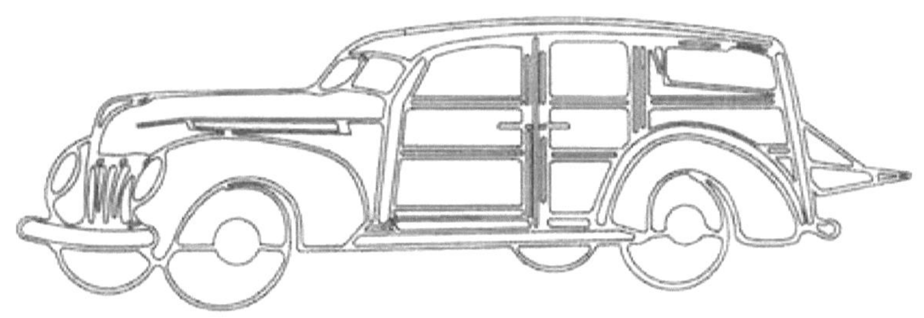

From East Los Angeles

During the 1950's

A Book of Fiction by Robert Nerbovig

Cover Art by Robert Nerbovig

solartoys@yahoo.com

Prologue

The hot California sun beat down on the cracked pavement of Brooklyn Avenue in East Los Angeles. Moe "Snake-Eyes" Juarez pulled his battered 1949 Ford Woody up to the curb, killing the engine with a sputter. He'd been driving these streets for over a decade, working cases from his cramped office above a noisy bakery.

As Juarez stepped out onto the sidewalk, he adjusted the brim of his fedora against the glare. This neighborhood had been his stomping grounds since the days of Prohibition back in the 1920s. A lot had changed since then, but the hustle and Code of the Streets remained the same.

Moe's beady eyes scanned the area, missing nothing. His nickname "Snake-Eyes" came from his keen eye for the dice during his gambling days. It was a skill that had kept him alive more times than he could count over his 10 years as a private eye.

A young Chicano kid watching from a nearby stoop eyed Juarez warily. "You the dick that got called about the Delgado case?" the youth asked, stubbing out a hand-rolled cigarette.

Juarez gave a curt nod. "That's right. What can you tell me about it?"

The kid smirked. "I might know a thing or two...if the price is right."

As he reached into his jacket for his wallet, Moe couldn't help but grin. Working the East L.A. streets - this was his life. No matter how tangled or dangerous the case, he always found a way to stick his nose in and uncover the truth.

Getting Even for Miguel

The California sun beat down mercilessly on Moe "Snake-Eyes" Juarez's fedora as he surveyed the scene. A knot of onlookers had gathered outside The Topper Club, a once-classy joint on Whittier Boulevard that had seen better days.

Yellow crime scene tape cordoned off the entrance, a stark contrast to the peeling red paint and chipped chrome accents on Moe's trusty 1949 Ford Woody parked across the street. He squinted through the ever-present cigarette smoke curling from the corner of his mouth, his eyes, as sharp as the nickname they earned him, taking in the details.

"What do we got Lou?" Moe grunted towards the young, uniformed officer guarding the entrance. Lou, barely out of his rookie year, looked relieved to see a familiar face.

"Stiff inside, Snake. Bartender, name's Miguel Rodriguez. Looks like he was roughed up pretty good before being iced." Lou explained, wiping sweat from his brow with a handkerchief. "No sign of forced entry, but the cash register's empty."

Moe pushed past the tape, the aged floorboards groaning under his weight. The smoky haze inside The Topper Club was thick enough to cut with a knife, a stale cocktail of cigarette smoke, spilled beer, and a faint undercurrent of something metallic. He knelt beside the body sprawled behind the bar. Miguel, a man built more for warmth than agility, lay crumpled amongst a mess of overturned bottles and a shattered shot glass. His face was a roadmap of bruises, a single, dark stain blooming on his starched white shirt.

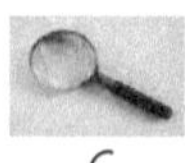

Moe's fingers danced across Miguel's neck, searching for a pulse that wasn't there. He stood, his keen eyes scanning the room. The Topper Club wasn't known for its highbrow clientele, but it wasn't exactly a gangster hangout either. More a blue-collar watering hole where folks drowned their sorrows or celebrated small victories. Who would want to hurt Miguel, and why?

A glint of gold caught his eye. Half-hidden beneath the bar, a worn photograph peeked out. He retrieved it carefully. The picture showed Miguel, a younger, happier version, standing with a woman with cascading dark hair and a mischievous grin. Scrawled on the back in faded ink were the words "My Celia, forever."

A lead, however thin, was better than nothing. This wasn't just about a robbery gone wrong. This was personal.

Moe tucked the photo into his pocket, the familiar weight of a new case settling in his gut. He wasn't just a private investigator; he was a weaver of stories, a mender of broken narratives. And Miguel Rodriguez's story, cut short behind the bar of his own dreams, was far from over. Snake-Eyes was on the case. The trail led Moe away from the glitz of Hollywood and into the labyrinthine alleys behind Whittier Boulevard. These were the forgotten corners of East LA, a tangled web of warehouses, flophouses, and smoky jazz clubs where shadows danced and secrets festered. His first stop was Celia's address scrawled on the back of the photo - a modest apartment building reeking of stale cabbage and despair.

The landlady, a woman with a permanent frown etched into her forehead and a cigarette perpetually dangling from her lips, informed Moe that Celia had moved

8

out months ago, leaving behind nothing but a trail of unpaid rent and a lingering air of melancholy. Undeterred, Moe pressed on, his inquiries leading him to a local jazz club called "The Blue Note." Word on the street was Celia had a voice like an angel dipped in whiskey, and a talent that could melt even the hardest of hearts.

The Blue Note was a dive bar in the truest sense of the word. The air hung thick with cigarette smoke and the melancholic strains of a saxophone. Moe sidled up to the bar, a worn fedora pulled low over his eyes, and ordered a shot of rye, the amber liquid burning a familiar path down his throat. He caught the bartender's eye, a wiry man with a handlebar mustache and a weary smile.

"Seen a dame around here," Moe began, his voice raspy from years of chain-smoking and countless whispered conversations.

"Beautiful gal, sings like a dream. Name's Celia Rodriguez."

The bartender's smile flickered. "Celia? Ain't seen her in a coon's age. Heard she got mixed up with the wrong crowd. Some outfit calling themselves 'The Aces.'"

The Aces. A notorious East LA gang known for shaking down local businesses and muscle for hire. A knot of worry tightened in Moe's gut. Celia tangled with gangsters? This wasn't the damsel in distress scenario he was expecting.

"What can you tell me about The Aces?" Moe pressed his gaze unwavering.

The bartender leaned in, his voice dropping to a conspiratorial whisper. "They run most of the rackets around here. Numbers games, protection money, the whole shebang. Heard they were after Miguel's bar for a while now. Maybe they got tired of asking nicely."

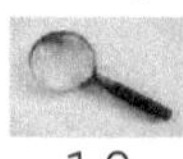

The pieces were starting to fall into place. The robbery, the murder, Celia's disappearance. It all pointed to The Aces, but their motive remained murky. Was it just a simple shakedown gone wrong, or was there something more sinister at play?

With a newfound urgency, Moe drained his glass and slapped a crumpled bill on the counter. The Blue Note held no more answers for now. It was time for a visit to The Aces' territory. He knew the risks, but one thing was certain: Snake-Eyes Juarez wasn't about to back down from a fight, especially when a woman's life, and the truth behind Miguel's death, hung in the balance.

Moe steered his trusty 1949 Ford Woody through the labyrinthine backstreets of East LA, the rhythmic clatter of its engine a steady counterpoint to the unease churning in his gut. The sun

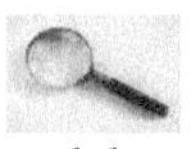

dipped lower in the sky, casting long shadows that stretched like grasping fingers across the decaying brick buildings. He was headed for a part of town known as "The Bottoms," a notorious Ace hangout riddled with chop shops, dive bars, and warehouses reeking of something far more nefarious than motor oil.

Parking his Woody in a dimly lit alley, far enough away to avoid unwanted attention, Moe donned a well-worn leather jacket, its pockets bulging with the tools of his trade - a trusty switchblade, a roll of nickels for payphones, and a crumpled wad of cash for well, let's just say unforeseen circumstances. He straightened his fedora, the fading palm tree embroidered on its band a reminder of a simpler time, and adjusted the cigarette dangling from his lips. It was showtime.

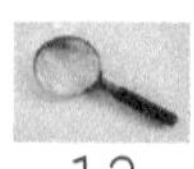

Following a network of informants and back-alley whispers, Moe located a ramshackle building adorned with a faded Ace of Spades insignia. Raucous laughter and the muffled thump of a bass line spilled out from within, a cacophony punctuated by the occasional clink of glasses. This was it - The Ace's den. Taking a deep drag from his cigarette, Moe flicked the spent ember into the shadows and steeled himself. He wasn't there to make friends.

He pushed open the creaking door, the stale air thick with the smell of cheap cigars and spilled whiskey. A dozen faces, a motley crew of thugs and lowlifes, swiveled towards him. The jukebox sputtered to a halt the silence broken only by the nervous hum of a flickering overhead bulb. All eyes were on the newcomer, the lone private investigator in a room full of vipers.

"Moe Juarez," he announced, his voice gravelly but firm. "Looking for some information."

A hulking figure with a shaved head and a cauliflower ear detached himself from the bar. This was Bruno, the Ace's muscle, his reputation for brutality preceding him. Bruno cracked his knuckles, a menacing sound that echoed in the tense silence.

"Information ain't free, pal," Bruno sneered, his voice dripping with menace. "What you got to offer?"

Moe met Bruno's gaze unflinchingly. "You got a dame named Celia Rodriguez here? She might be worth something to you, but she's worth a lot more to me."

A ripple of surprise ran through the room. Bruno's scowl deepened. "Celia? Ain't seen her around. You sure you got the right place, old timer?"

Moe knew Bruno was lying. He could smell it, a potent mix of sweat, fear, and something far more sinister. He needed to tread carefully, a wrong move here could get him seriously hurt, or worse.

"Look," Moe said, tossing a wad of cash on the bar. "Double what you usually squeeze out of a joint like Miguel's. Just tell me where Celia is, and we can all walk away happy."

Bruno eyed the money with avarice, then glanced towards a doorway at the back of the room. A figure emerged from the shadows, a tall, lean man with a cruel glint in his eyes. This was Frankie "The Ace" Russo, the undisputed leader of the gang.

"Let him talk, Bruno," Russo drawled, his voice smooth as polished marble but laced with a hidden threat. "Maybe this old buzzard has something interesting to say."

Intrigued, Moe took a cautious step forward. He wasn't sure what he was walking into, but one thing was clear - the deeper he dug, the murkier the waters became. Celia was alive, that much he knew. But whether she was a willing guest of The Aces or a captive in their clutches remained a chilling mystery. And Moe Juarez, with his unwavering gaze and a steely resolve, was determined to find out.

The air crackled with tension as Moe stared down Frankie "The Ace" Russo. Bruno, still fuming over the crumpled bills on the bar, shifted his weight menacingly.

"Alright, buzzard," Frankie drawled, a cruel amusement flickering in his eyes. "You got guts for an old timer. Spill it. What's your connection to Celia?"

Moe, never one to back down from a challenge, took a long drag from his

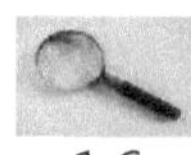

16

cigarette, letting the smoke curl around him like a battle cry. "Let's just say her safety is important to me. And right now, that safety seems to be in jeopardy with you fine gentlemen."

Frankie's smile vanished. "Jeopardy? You think you can walk in here, flash some cash, and threaten The Aces? We control this town, old man. Nobody crosses us and gets away with it."

A tense silence followed, broken only by the dripping of a leaky faucet somewhere in the back. Moe knew he couldn't bluff his way out of this. He needed to play a different card.

"Alright, let's rephrase this," Moe said, his voice dropping to a conspiratorial whisper. "Instead of Celia, how about Miguel's bar? You boys having any trouble collecting your 'protection money' lately?"

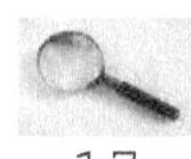

Frankie's eyes narrowed. Bruno snorted a sound suspiciously close to a laugh.

"We own half that damn bar," Bruno growled. "What's your point?"

Moe leaned closer, his voice barely above a murmur. "Maybe there's something Miguel wasn't telling you. Something valuable hidden away. Something worth more than a few measly protection payments."

Intrigue flickered in Frankie's eyes. Money talks, even to a notorious gangster. Here was a new angle, a potential windfall they hadn't considered.

"What kind of valuable?" Frankie asked, his voice devoid of its earlier amusement.

Moe shrugged, feigning nonchalance. "Could be anything. Maybe some old war bonds, a stash of uncut diamonds, even a secret recipe for the best damn margaritas this side of the border."

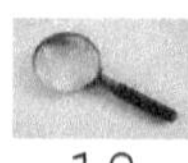

Bruno scoffed, but Frankie remained silent, considering Moe's words.

"Proof?" Frankie challenged finally.

Moe knew he was pushing his luck, but the desperation in Celia's eyes from the photo flashed in his mind. "No proof," he admitted. "Just a hunch. But if you boys let me talk to Celia, maybe she can shed some light on the matter."

The room remained quiet. Bruno's knuckles cracked ominously. The fate of Moe, and potentially Celia, hung in the balance.

The air in the dingy Ace hangout felt thick enough to chew on. Bruno loomed like a menacing thundercloud, his every twitch a potential prelude to violence. Frankie "The Ace" Russo, however, remained a puzzle. His face, usually a mask of callous amusement, was now etched with a mix of suspicion and something akin to curiosity.

"Talk to Celia?" Frankie echoed, his voice a low rumble. "Why should we trust you, old man?"

"Because," Moe countered, his voice steady despite the knot of worry tightening in his gut, "a dead Miguel ain't good for business. You scare the other saps into submission, but a stiff on your doorstep? That attracts unwanted attention."

It was a gamble, playing on Frankie's fear of the law. But it seemed to resonate. A flicker of annoyance crossed Bruno's face, a silent acknowledgment of the truth in Moe's words.

"Alright, buzzard," Frankie finally conceded, a hint of a smirk playing on his lips. "You got yourself a deal. But if this is some kind of setup..." he trailed off, letting the unspoken threat hang heavy in the air.

Bruno, with a none-too-gentle shove, ushered Moe towards a dimly lit back room. The floorboards creaked ominously under their weight. The air grew colder, the stale scent of cigarettes replaced by a metallic tang that sent shivers down Moe's spine.

The back room was bare except for a single bare bulb hanging from the ceiling, casting long, grotesque shadows on the wall. In the center, a lone figure sat hunched over in a rickety chair. As Moe's eyes adjusted, a gasp escaped his lips.

It was Celia. But not the vibrant woman he'd seen in the photograph. Her face was pale and drawn, her eyes filled with a haunted fear. Her once-flowing dark hair was matted and dirty, a stark contrast to the once-elegant dress now hanging limply on her thin frame.

"Celia?" Moe breathed, his voice thick with concern.

Celia's head snapped up, her eyes widening in recognition. A flicker of hope, quickly extinguished by a flicker of fear, danced across her features.

"Mr. Juarez?" she rasped, her voice barely a whisper. "What are you doing here?"

Before Moe could answer, Bruno shoved him roughly into the chair opposite Celia. The metallic tang in the air grew stronger. Moe glanced around, finally noticing a glint of metal on a nearby table - a hypodermic needle, filled with a clear liquid.

"This dame ain't talkin'," Bruno growled, his voice laced with frustration. "Maybe you can loosen her tongue, old man. Just make sure she spills everything about Miguel's little secret stash."

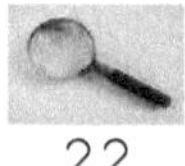

With that ominous statement, Bruno slammed the door shut, plunging the room into an eerie darkness. Moe was trapped with a frightened woman, a loaded syringe, and a gang of ruthless criminals baying for blood. The simple case of a murdered bartender had taken a sharp turn into a desperate fight for survival. And Snake-Eyes Juarez, with his back against the wall, knew this was just the beginning.

Panic clawed at Moe's throat, but he forced it down. He needed a clear head, not just for himself, but for Celia. The sickly-sweet scent of the liquid in the syringe sent a tremor through him. They were serious about making her talk.

"Celia," he said softly, his voice cutting through the oppressive silence. "Don't worry, I'm here to help."

He could barely see her face in the darkness, but the tremor in her voice

when she replied confirmed his worst fear. "They'll kill me," she whispered, "If I don't tell them..." Her voice trailed off, choked with fear.

"Tell them what?" Moe pressed gently, his mind racing for a plan. He needed to buy time, distract Bruno and Frankie, long enough to figure a way out.

"Miguel…" Celia began, then stopped abruptly as a muffled thump echoed from the hallway outside. They both listened, hearts hammering against their ribs. Another thump, followed by a string of curses.

"Sounds like Bruno's having trouble with someone," Moe murmured, hope flickering in his chest. Maybe, just maybe, this was a chance.

"Celia," he continued, his voice low and urgent. "Do you know anything about a secret stash? Anything Miguel might have hidden?"

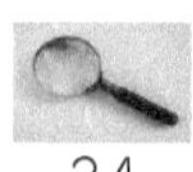

Celia hesitated, then shook her head. "No. There was nothing like that. Miguel just wanted to run his bar, have a little peace."

Moe believed her. The desperation in her voice, the fear in her eyes - it wasn't an act. But he needed Frankie to believe it too. An idea sparked in his mind, a desperate gamble.

"Then we need to convince them of that," he said, his voice hardening with resolve. "We need to give them what they want, even if it's a lie."

Celia stared at him, confused. "But how?"

Moe took a deep breath. "We improvise, Celia. We play their game, but we play it smart." He explained his plan in a hushed whisper, a risky proposition that hinged on Celia's cooperation and a little bit of luck.

The clatter outside grew louder, punctuated by Bruno's increasingly frustrated shouts. Time was running out. Celia, after a moment's hesitation, nodded her agreement. Desperation can be a powerful motivator.

Just as the heavy oak door creaked open, revealing a furious Bruno, Moe slammed his fist on the table, sending the syringe clattering to the floor.

"Alright, you win!" he bellowed, his voice rough with anger. "Celia finally remembered. There is a stash, but it's not at the bar. It's…" He paused dramatically, letting the suspense hang in the air. " Hidden in a safety deposit box at the First National Bank!"

Bruno's eyes widened. Greed momentarily eclipsed his scowl. "Safety deposit box, huh? What's the combination?"

Moe glanced at Celia, a silent plea for her to follow his lead. She took a shaky

breath, then met Bruno's gaze with a fabricated defiance.

"He never told me" She said, her voice trembling slightly. "He said it was a surprise for our anniversary. But I can get the box open if you take me to the bank!"

Bruno considered this for a long moment, his gaze flickering between them. Moe held his breath, willing the gangster to buy their story.

Finally, with a grunt, Bruno seemed to accept it. "Alright," he conceded, shoving a gun into Moe's hand. "You two come with me. And if this is some kind of trick..." He didn't need to finish the threat. The icy glint in his eyes spoke volumes.

Moe and Celia exchanged a tense glance. They were far from free. The bank was a gamble, a desperate move that could backfire spectacularly. But for now,

they were alive. And as Snake-Eyes Juarez well knew, in the game of survival, sometimes even a bad bet was better than no bet at all. Their perilous journey to the First National Bank, with a gun pointed at their backs and a lie hanging over their heads, had just begun.

The roar of Bruno's muscle car cleaved through the night, a discordant symphony against the backdrop of chirping crickets and the distant wail of a police siren. Moe, his knuckles white from gripping the pistol shoved into his hand, stole a glance at Celia huddled beside him. Her face, pale under the sickly glow of the dashboard lights, was a mask of forced composure.

"We gotta stick to the plan," Moe whispered, his voice barely audible over the engine's rumble.

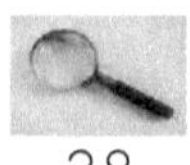

Celia offered a shaky nod, her eyes welling up with a mixture of fear and a flicker of defiance. Moe admired her courage. He'd seen hardened criminals crumble under pressure, but Celia, a woman caught in the crosshairs of a ruthless gang, was holding her own.

Bruno, a hulking silhouette in the driver's seat, remained silent, his focus on navigating the dimly lit streets. Every turn they took felt like a roll of the dice. One wrong move, one unexpected encounter, and their fragile facade of cooperation could shatter.

As they approached the gleaming facade of the First National Bank, tension crackled in the air like static electricity. Bruno pulled the car to a halt across the street, the engine sputtering to a disgruntled cough.

"Alright, you two," Bruno growled, his voice gravelly. "Remember what you're

gonna say. One wrong word, and this little reunion turns into a permanent one."

Moe swallowed hard, the metallic tang of fear coating his tongue. He had a feeling Bruno wasn't bluffing. Their lie, while seemingly convincing, had a gaping hole - they didn't have a box number, let alone a key. Reaching the bank was just the first step. Now, they needed a way to improvise, to buy enough time to formulate an escape plan.

"Don't worry," Moe said, his voice surprisingly steady. "Celia will handle it." He wasn't sure if he was reassuring Bruno or himself.

Celia, taking a deep breath, stepped out of the car, her legs trembling slightly. With a practiced smile, she approached the lone security guard patrolling the bank's entrance. The guard, a bored-looking teenager with a thick wad of gum

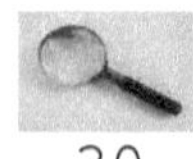

permanently lodged in his cheek, eyed her suspiciously.

"Evening, ma'am," he mumbled, barely glancing up from a comic book tucked under his arm. "Bank's closed."

Celia, her voice laced with a hint of manufactured urgency, explained their fabricated story about the safety deposit box and the "forgotten" anniversary surprise. The guard, initially skeptical, seemed swayed by Celia's apparent distress.

"Hold on," he mumbled, scratching his head with the butt of his flashlight. "Technically, the bank's closed… but Mr. Henderson, the manager, is still here finishing some paperwork. He might be able to help – for a fee, of course."

A glimmer of hope flickered in Moe's chest. A "fee" could be negotiated. Maybe, just maybe, this unexpected twist could work to their advantage. As Celia,

with practiced charm, engaged the guard
in conversation, Moe leaned back in the
car, his mind racing. He needed to
think, to find a way out of this
precarious situation.
Suddenly, a glint of metal caught his
eye. It was the discarded safety deposit
box key photocopied and tucked inside
Miguel's picture with Celia. The key in
the photo was worn, with a distinctive
inscription on its handle - a tiny palm
tree. An idea, audacious and risky,
began to take shape in Moe's mind. He
reached into his pocket, his fingers
brushing against the worn photograph. A
desperate gamble, but in the world of
Snake-Eyes Juarez, sometimes desperate
was the only option.
The flickering neon sign above the First
National Bank cast an eerie glow on Moe's
face as he watched Celia weave her tale
with the security guard. A bead of sweat

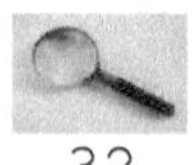

trickled down his temple, the cool night air doing little to quell the nervous fire burning in his gut. Everything hinged on this next move.

He discreetly fished Miguel's photo out of his pocket, the worn image a stark reminder of the stakes. Turning it over, he focused on the key – the tiny palm tree on its handle a beacon of hope in the darkness. With a silent prayer, he tore the photo along the crease, carefully separating the key image from Miguel and Celia's faces.

Just then, Celia's voice cut through the tension. "Mr. Henderson? He'd be willing to help for a price?" Her voice, though laced with forced cheer, held a hint of desperation.

The guard, a sucker for a pretty face and a well-told sob story, nodded eagerly. "Sure thing, ma'am. Just gotta convince Mr. Henderson it's worth his trouble."

He puffed out his chest, a picture of misplaced authority.

"Consider it convinced," Moe said, stepping out of the car, the photo scrap held tight in his hand. "And here's a little extra incentive." He flashed a wad of cash, the crumpled bills a far cry from the kind of money The Aces probably dealt with, but enough, hopefully, to pique the guard's greed.

The guard's eyes widened. His gaze flickered between the money and Moe, then back to Celia. A silent debate played out on his face between duty and temptation.

"Alright, alright," he finally conceded, a hint of a smirk playing on his lips. "Let's see what Mr. Henderson has to say."

Relief washed over Moe, a temporary reprieve in a life-or-death situation. He slipped the photo scrap into his

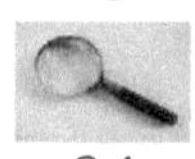

pocket, a secret weapon in his unfolding plan. He wasn't sure what awaited them inside the bank, but he knew one thing for sure - they weren't there to access a safety deposit box. They were there to get out, and getting out meant taking a calculated risk.

As they entered the bank, the sterile atmosphere felt suffocating after the gritty streets. Mr. Henderson, a portly man with thinning hair and a perpetual frown, looked up from his desk with a mixture of annoyance and curiosity. The guard launched into a garbled explanation, punctuated by nervous glances at Moe and Celia.

"Lost key, sentimental value, anniversary surprise," Mr. Henderson droned, unimpressed. He eyed them all with suspicion. "This better not be some kind of scam."

Moe's voice was calm despite the tremor in his hand. "No scam, sir. Just a desperate situation. Look, here's the box number," he lied, pulling out a random slip of paper from his pocket. "And while we can't find the key, maybe there's a way you can help us access the box with a special tool?"

Mr. Henderson's frown deepened. "Special tool? What kind of special tool are we talking about?"

Taking a gamble, Moe reached into his pocket once more, his heart pounding against his ribs. He pulled out the photo scrap, the tiny palm tree gleaming under the harsh fluorescent lights.

"Something like this," he said, holding it up. "Maybe a master key with a similar design?"

Mr. Henderson's eyes narrowed as he scrutinized the photo scrap. A flicker of recognition crossed his face. "That

looks like the old locksmith's key," he muttered, stroking his chin thoughtfully. "Haven't seen one of those in years. But…" he trailed off, his gaze shifting towards the vault door behind him.

The air hung thick with tension. Had Moe's outlandish plan backfired? Or had he, by chance, stumbled upon a loophole? Mr. Henderson's gaze lingered on the photo scrap in Moe's hand, his face a mask of contemplation. A bead of sweat trickled down Moe's temple, the silence stretching into an eternity. Had his desperate gamble landed them in hotter water, or had he, by some stroke of luck, stumbled into an unexpected advantage?

"That old key," Mr. Henderson finally rumbled, breaking the silence. "It used to belong to Mr. Harris, the locksmith we used before the fancy digital codes came along. Haven't seen it since he retired." He squinted at the photo, then back at Moe. "But that palm tree looks awfully familiar."

A surge of hope jolted through Moe. Perhaps the key wasn't just a random image from Miguel's past, but a forgotten connection with the bank itself. He pressed his advantage.

"Maybe," Moe ventured, his voice carefully neutral, "there's a chance someone here still has access to a similar key. Someone who could help us access the box, for a fee of course."

Mr. Henderson's lips twitched into a sly smile. "Well, I wouldn't say access, but…" he glanced towards the vault door once more, a calculating glint in his eyes. "There might be a way to nudge the lock open just a smidge. Enough for someone nimble to reach inside, retrieve their anniversary surprise."

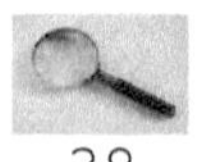

The air crackled with a silent negotiation. Mr. Henderson, clearly tempted by the offered cash, was weighing the risk against the potential reward. Meanwhile, Bruno, simmering with suspicion in the corner, eyed the unfolding scene with growing impatience. "How much is this 'nudge' gonna cost us?" Celia asked, her voice tight but steady. Mr. Henderson named a sum that made Moe's wallet wince, but considering the alternative, it seemed like a bargain. He readily agreed, the wad of cash exchanging hands with a satisfying rustle.

Bruno, however, was not as easily appeased. He stomped forward, his face a thundercloud. "What's taking so long? Let's get this damn box open and get outta here!"

Before Mr. Henderson could respond, a high-pitched whine pierced the air. The

bank's security alarm, triggered by either the guard's carelessness or the suspicious activity, wailed like a banshee.

Panic flooded the room. Mr. Henderson swore under his breath. Bruno's hand flew to his gun, his eyes blazing with fury. Celia let out a gasp, her carefully constructed facade crumbling. Moe, however, saw an opportunity in the chaos. He grabbed Celia's arm, his voice a low growl. "Now!" He shoved her towards the back entrance he'd spotted earlier, a fire escape emblazoned with a bright red "No Exit" sign.

Chaos erupted. Bruno, momentarily stunned, bellowed a curse. Mr. Henderson dove under his desk. The security guard, his face pale with fear, froze like a deer in headlights.

Seizing the moment, Moe followed Celia towards the fire escape. He could hear

Bruno's enraged shouts behind him, followed by the pounding of heavy footsteps. Adrenaline surged through his veins, propelling him forward.

Reaching the fire escape, they scrambled down the rickety metal steps, the harsh clang echoing in the night. Distant sirens wailed, growing louder with each passing second.

The cool night air whipped at Moe's face as they landed in a dark alley. He glanced back, his heart hammering against his ribs. No sign of Bruno or the security guard. They had escaped, for now.

"This way," Celia gasped, grabbing his hand and pulling him deeper into the labyrinthine alleyways. They ran, their lungs burning, their legs screaming in protest. But they didn't dare stop. Not until they were far, far away from the First National Bank, the botched plan,

and the ruthless gangster with a vendetta.

As they finally stumbled to a halt, hidden in the shadows of a forgotten warehouse, the adrenaline rush began to fade, replaced by a bone-deep exhaustion. They had survived, but at what cost?

Celia leaned against the rough brick wall, her face streaked with tears and soot. "We did it, Mr. Juarez," she whispered, her voice trembling. "We escaped."

Moe nodded his own body wracked with fatigue. But a sense of accomplishment, however hollow, flickered in his chest. He had saved Celia, at least for now. The mystery of Miguel's death, however, remained unsolved. And the question of The Aces' hidden motives hung heavy.

Moe slumped against the grimy brick wall, the dampness seeping through his clothes and chilling him to the bone. Exhaustion finally caught up to him, a heavy mantle settling on his aching muscles. He stole a glance at Celia, huddled beside him, her face a mask of conflicting emotions - relief, fear, and a flicker of gratitude that warmed him more than any stolen heat.

"We did it," she repeated, her voice barely a whisper. "We got away."

"For now," Moe corrected gently. He knew the reprieve was temporary. Bruno wouldn't give up easily. The man craved control, and their escape was a stinging slap in the face. They needed a plan, a way to disappear into the city's labyrinthine underbelly, a place where even a notorious gangster like The Ace had trouble reaching.

"There's gotta be a reason they wanted you to lie about the safety deposit box," Celia said, her voice laced with a newfound determination. "Maybe that's

the key to figuring out what happened to Miguel."

Moe considered this. Bruno's relentless pursuit of a non-existent safety deposit box did seem peculiar. Why go to such lengths for something that didn't exist? Unless, of course, there was something else at play. Something Miguel had stumbled upon, something The Aces desperately wanted to keep hidden.

"There's something else they're after," Moe muttered, the pieces of the puzzle slowly starting to click into place. "Something connected to Miguel, something valuable enough to risk getting caught on camera at a bank."

The memory of the photo scrap, the worn key with the tiny palm tree, sparked a new line of thought. Perhaps it wasn't just a random image from Miguel's past, but a clue, a forgotten connection. Maybe the key wasn't meant for a safety

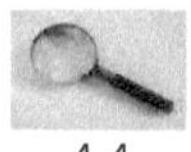

deposit box at all, but for something else entirely.

"Miguel was a good man," Celia continued, her voice catching in her throat. "He wouldn't have gotten involved with anything shady willingly. We need to find out what this is all about."

As the first rays of dawn painted the sky in soft hues of orange and pink, casting an ethereal glow on the grimy alleyway, a new resolve hardened in Moe's eyes. He wouldn't let Miguel's death be a footnote in the city's crime ledger. He wouldn't let Celia, a woman caught in the crossfire, become another victim. He would find answers, even if it meant diving deeper into the murky waters of East LA's criminal underworld.

Their first order of business was disappearing. Moe knew a few safe houses scattered around the city, havens for those on the run, discreet havens run by

individuals who owed him favors, ghosts of past cases. He would contact Mickey "The Mouth" Malone, a former informant with a network of contacts and a penchant for gossip. Mickey might not be trustworthy, but he knew where the whispers originated, who held the keys to the city's secrets, for the right price. Reaching Mickey's dilapidated apartment, a dingy building perpetually shrouded in the stench of stale beer and regret, was half the battle. The rest involved navigating Mickey's paranoia, a finely honed skill honed by years of double-crossing and dodging bullets. Finally, after a tense negotiation fueled by cheap whiskey and broken promises, Moe secured Mickey's "assistance."

"The Aces," Mickey slurred, his bloodshot eyes gleaming with a hint of mischief. "Big trouble. Messing with the wrong crowd. Heard whispers about a shipment,

something big. Drugs, maybe guns, something that'll line Frankie's pockets and ruffle feathers with a few important people."

Drugs and guns explained the violence surrounding Miguel. But why was a safety deposit box such a crucial part of the equation? Was it a ledger, a list of contacts, or something more?

"Safety deposit box," Mickey continued, his voice trailing off into a drunken mumble. "Rumor mill says it holds the key to the whole operation. Some kinda proof, a blackmail chip, who knows? Frankie's been tight-lipped, but his boys are getting sloppy."

Blackmail. That explained The Aces' relentless pursuit of a non-existent box. They were desperate to silence Miguel before he could expose them. But to whom? Who were the "important people" Mickey mentioned?

The answer, they realized, might lie in Miguel's past. Who were his friends? Who might he have confided in, someone with the power to bring down an organization like The Aces?

Their investigation led them down a dusty trail of memories. They spoke to Miguel's bar patrons, a motley crew of dockworkers, washed-up actors, and a surprisingly chatty librarian with a penchant for classic noir novels. Each conversation yielded a new piece of the puzzle, a blurry snapshot of Miguel's life beyond the bar.

There was Rosie, the gruff but kind waitress with a heart of gold. She told them about Miguel's late-night meetings with a well-dressed man, a lawyer by the name of Thomas Walsh, a name that sent shivers down Moe's spine. Walsh was known for representing influential clients, the kind who swam in the murky

waters of city politics and organized crime. Could Miguel have stumbled upon something Walsh was trying to bury? Their search led them to Walsh's opulent office, a stark contrast to the seedy underbelly they'd navigated so far. Walsh, a man with a steely gaze and a smile that never quite reached his eyes, listened to their story with a practiced air of aloofness.

"Miguel Juarez?" he scoffed, steepling his manicured fingers. "A good bartender, nothing more. I had a few drinks with the man, but our conversations never strayed beyond the weather and the latest baseball game." His denial hung heavy in the air, laced with a subtle threat. Leaving Walsh's office, Moe knew they wouldn't get any answers from the lawyer directly. They needed leverage, a way to crack his carefully constructed facade.

Back in Mickey's grimy haven, fueled by stale coffee and suspicion, a plan began to take shape. They needed something to force Walsh's hand, a bargaining chip to pry open the locked doors of his secrets. Their eyes fell on the photo scrap – the worn key with the palm tree.

A flicker of recognition sparked in Mickey's bloodshot eyes. "That key" he mumbled, scratching his unkempt beard. "It looks familiar. Like something my old man used to carry around. Said it belonged to his locksmith buddy, a guy named… Harris, yeah, that's it, Mr. Harris."

The name echoed in Moe's mind. Mr. Henderson, the bank manager, had mentioned the same name, the retired locksmith with the key that looked suspiciously like the one in Miguel's photo. Could there be a connection?

Seeking out Mr. Henderson was a gamble. After all, the man had aided their escape, a risky move that could have landed him in hot water with Bruno and The Aces. But they needed answers, and Mr. Henderson, with his peculiar knowledge of forgotten keys, might hold the missing piece.

The retired locksmith lived in a quiet suburban neighborhood, a stark contrast to the seedy underbelly they frequented. He greeted them with a mixture of surprise and apprehension, his eyes widening at the sight of the photo scrap. "The palm tree key," he muttered, his voice laced with nostalgia. "That belonged to a special lockbox. A box I built for a client back in the day, a man named Walsh, Thomas Walsh to be precise." The revelation hit them like a freight train. The key wasn't for a safety deposit box at all, but for a custom-

built lockbox in Walsh's possession. A lockbox that likely held the incriminating evidence Miguel had stumbled upon - evidence that could bring down The Aces and expose Walsh's shady dealings.

Fueled by renewed purpose, they returned to Walsh's office, this time armed with the key and a newfound determination. Walsh, his facade crumbling under the weight of their accusations, finally confessed.

Miguel, it turned out, had overheard a conversation between Walsh and a high-ranking official within the city's powerful dockworker's union. The conversation detailed a scheme to funnel illegal goods through the docks, a scheme that lined Walsh's pockets and kept the union in control.

Miguel, a man with a strong moral compass, had threatened to expose the operation. Walsh, fearing his career and freedom, had silenced him permanently. The safety deposit box was a carefully crafted lie, a smokescreen to divert attention from the real evidence locked away in the custom box.

The revelation brought a wave of anger and grief crashing down on Moe and Celia. Miguel, a good man caught in the crossfire of greed and corruption. But their fight wasn't over. They had the evidence, the truth that could bring Walsh and his co-conspirators to justice. Navigating the treacherous waters of city politics proved to be a whole new battle. The police, some of them on the union's payroll, were skeptical at first. But with the weight of undeniable evidence and a tenacious reporter sniffing out the story, the tide began to turn.

The scandal erupted like a volcanic eruption. Newspapers blared headlines about corruption, arrests were made and Walsh, stripped of his power and reputation, became a pariah within the legal community. The dockworker's union, its leadership decimated, faced a long road to reform. Yet, the victory tasted bittersweet.

Justice for Miguel, though served, couldn't erase the gaping hole left in their lives. Celia, with a heavy heart, sold the bar, the once vibrant space now echoing with the ghosts of laughter and stolen glances. Moe, adrift without a case or a clear purpose, drifted back to his usual haunts, the familiar anonymity of the city a strange comfort.

One rainy afternoon, hunched over a lukewarm coffee in a greasy spoon diner, a familiar voice broke through the haze. It was Mickey, his eyes a little less bloodshot, his demeanor a touch less paranoid. He slid into the booth across from Moe, a manila envelope clutched in his hand.

"Heard you were laying low," Mickey rasped, his voice rough. "Figured you might be interested in this."

He pushed the envelope across the table. Inside, nestled amongst faded newspaper clippings, was a worn driver's license - Miguel's name and picture staring back at them. But on the back, scribbled in a hurried hand, was an address - a location outside the city limits.

"Found it at my old man's place," Mickey explained. "Cleaning out the attic, found a box filled with his old case files. Seems your buddy Miguel had a secret life, one he kept close to the vest."

A spark of curiosity ignited within Moe. Miguel, a man seemingly content with

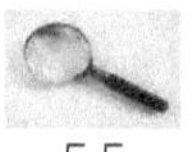

running a bar, harboring a secret? The implications sent shivers down his spine. Could this be another chapter in the story, a hidden thread leading them down an unknown path?

"Let's check it out," Moe muttered, a flicker of his old fire returning to his eyes. He couldn't shake the feeling that Miguel's death was more than just a gangland hit. This address, this forgotten secret, might be the key to unraveling a whole new mystery, one that could pull them back into the heart of danger.

As they drove towards the unknown address, a storm raged outside, mirroring the turmoil within Moe. He knew this path wouldn't be easy. New dangers, new enemies, could lurk around the corner. But the memory of Miguel, his kind eyes and unwavering sense of justice, fueled Moe's resolve. He wouldn't let his

friend's secrets remain buried. He wouldn't let Miguel become another forgotten face in the city's unforgiving streets.

The address led them to a dilapidated cabin nestled deep in the woods, its windows boarded up, its paint peeling like sunburnt skin. An unsettling silence hung heavy in the air, broken only by the relentless drumming of rain on the corrugated metal roof.

A sense of foreboding washed over them, but there was no turning back now. Moe, with a deep breath and a hand on his trusty switchblade, cautiously pushed open the creaking door. The stale smell of dust and mildew hit them first, followed by a darkness so thick it seemed to swallow the light from their flashlights.

As they ventured deeper, the cabin revealed its secrets – dusty maps,

cryptic notes scrawled on yellowed paper, and a hidden compartment behind a loose floorboard. Inside, nestled amongst old photographs and faded receipts, lay a worn leather-bound journal.

By the flickering light of their flashlights, they began to read. The journal, meticulously kept by Miguel, detailed his investigation into a series of missing persons cases, all seemingly unconnected drifters who vanished without a trace. His investigation led him to this remote location, to a rumor of a hidden mine, and a ruthless organization exploiting undocumented workers within its depths.

A cold dread settled in Moe's stomach. Miguel hadn't just stumbled upon a simple corruption scheme. He had uncovered something far more sinister, something that cost him his life. And now, Moe and Celia were standing at the precipice of

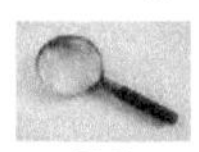

a terrifying truth, one that could put them in the crosshairs of a deadly conspiracy.

With the storm raging outside and a chilling secret unveiled within the cabin walls, Moe knew their journey had just taken a dramatic turn. The fight for justice for Miguel had transformed into a fight for survival. They were about to step into a world of darkness, greed, and exploitation, a world where the stakes couldn't be higher. And for Moe Juarez, the man who walked the line between right and wrong, there was no turning back.

The rain had subsided by morning, leaving the world outside the cabin scrubbed clean and glistening. Inside, a tense silence hung in the air as Moe and Celia finished reading Miguel's journal. The weight of his discovery, the chilling reality of what he'd stumbled upon, pressed down on them both.

Celia, her voice tight with fear, broke the silence first. "A hidden mine, forced labor this is bigger than we could have ever imagined. These people, whoever they are, won't hesitate to silence anyone who gets too close."

Moe nodded his jaw clenched tight. He knew she was right. But backing down wasn't an option. Miguel wouldn't have turned away, wouldn't have allowed such an injustice to continue. They had stumbled into this, but now they had a responsibility to see it through.

"We need a plan," Moe said, his voice gruff. He spread the maps and notes across the creaky wooden table, Miguel's meticulous handwriting outlining the location of the mine and the surrounding area.

Their first priority was information. They needed to understand the scope of the operation, the number of people

60

involved, and the best way to approach the mine without alerting those running it. Miguel's entries hinted at a contact a local journalist named Sarah Miller who had been investigating similar disappearances.

"We find Miller," Moe said, pointing to a faded newspaper clipping with her picture attached. "She might have some leads, some way to get us close to the mine without getting ourselves killed."

Packing the journal, maps, and any other potentially useful items from the cabin, a sense of urgency pulsed through them. They couldn't afford to waste time. Leaving the cabin behind, they retraced their steps back to the city, the weight of their newfound knowledge heavy in their hearts.

Their search for Sarah Miller led them down a labyrinthine path through the city's underbelly. Following whispers

and dead ends, they finally found her holed up in a dilapidated apartment, surrounded by stacks of newspapers and half-empty coffee cups. A woman with fiery red hair and a gaze that could pierce steel, Sarah greeted them with a mixture of skepticism and curiosity.

After explaining their connection to Miguel and his investigation, Sarah's initial suspicion melted away, replaced by a grim determination. She too had been investigating the disappearances, facing threats and dead ends at every turn. Miguel's journal provided a missing piece, a crucial link that could lead them closer to the truth.

"The mine," Sarah muttered, tracing a finger across the map. "It's located on private property owned by a ruthless corporation called 'Horizon Resources.' They're a powerful outfit, with fingers in all sorts of dirty businesses."

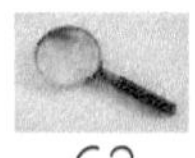

The name sent a shiver down Moe's spine. Horizon Resources was a known entity, a corporation with a reputation for environmental transgressions and unethical labor practices. But forced labor and disappearances? That ventured into a whole new level of criminal activity.

"We need proof," Moe said, his voice hardening. "Something concrete to expose what's happening at that mine. Without evidence, it's just another conspiracy theory."

Sarah nodded, a glint of determination in her eyes. "I have a source," she confessed. "Someone on the inside, a disgruntled ex-employee who witnessed some pretty horrific stuff. He's willing to talk, but only if we can guarantee his safety."

Getting close to the mine and securing the evidence was a risky operation. They

needed a plan, a way to infiltrate the heavily guarded perimeter and retrieve the information they needed. The source wouldn't be able to leave his post, so they needed a way to get in, gather evidence, and disappear before anyone was the wiser.

Days turned into weeks as they meticulously crafted their operation. Moe, drawing on his experience navigating the city's criminal underworld, secured fake IDs and a stolen truck. Sarah, leveraging her network of contacts, obtained blueprints of the mine's layout and security protocols. Celia, with her keen eye for detail, devised a plan for retrieving the evidence while minimizing their risks.

The night of the infiltration arrived a dark canvas painted with the threat of danger. Armed with their plan, their borrowed identities, and a healthy dose

of desperation, they set off towards the Horizon Resources property. As they neared the mine's perimeter, a nervous silence hung heavy in the air. This was the point of no return.

The headlights of the stolen truck cut through the inky blackness, carving a temporary path through the dense forest surrounding the Horizon Resources property. The air hung heavy with the scent of pine and damp earth, the only sounds the rhythmic rumble of the engine and the nervous drumming of their hearts. Moe gripped the steering wheel, knuckles white. Beside him, Sarah, her fiery hair pulled back in a tight bun, scanned the approaching tree line with a practiced eye. In the back, Celia, a bundle of nervous energy, checked and rechecked the duffel bag containing their makeshift camera equipment. Tonight, they were more than just a bartender, a journalist,

and a grieving friend. Tonight, they were a ragtag team of vigilantes, determined to expose the horrors hidden within the walls of the Horizon Mine.

The pre-dawn light revealed a sprawling complex of buildings, industrial monstrosities spewing plumes of black smoke into the polluted sky. A chain-link fence, topped with razor wire and patrolled by unseen guards with attack dogs, marked the perimeter. Their stolen truck, a beat-up Ford with a dubious paint job, wouldn't get them past the main gate.

"Here's the drop-off point," Sarah said, pointing to a barely visible dirt road branching off the main path. "The source said there's an abandoned ranger station about a half-mile in. That's where we'll stage the operation."

Following the bumpy road, they navigated the treacherous terrain, the headlights bouncing erratically over potholes and fallen branches. Finally, they reached the clearing Sarah described. The ranger station, a ramshackle wooden structure with peeling paint and broken windows, loomed before them, a silent testament to the neglect that mirrored the corporation's disregard for human life. Inside, the air was stale and thick with the smell of mildew. Using flashlights, they surveyed the dusty interior, transforming the abandoned station into their temporary base of operations. Celia, with surprising dexterity, set up the camera equipment – a small, high-resolution device Sarah had procured, hidden within a seemingly innocuous birdwatcher's backpack.

"Alright, listen up," Moe said, his voice low and serious. "We have one shot at

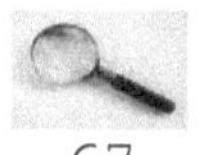

67

this. Sarah, you'll be on lookout,
keeping an eye on the perimeter and any
patrols. Celia, you'll be stationed near
the ventilation shaft, the source said
it's a weak point in the security system.
Once I get close enough, you'll activate
the camera and start recording."
His gaze met Celia's, a silent exchange
of unspoken fears and unwavering resolve.
"Remember," he continued, his voice a
touch softer, "our goal is to get the
evidence and get out clean. Don't
hesitate to pull me back if things go
south."
Celia nodded, her eyes welling up with a
mix of fear and determination. They
weren't soldiers, nor were they
professional operatives. They were
ordinary people caught in an
extraordinary situation, driven by a
fierce sense of justice and the memory of
a lost friend.

The pre-dawn light began to filter through the cracked windows, casting long, skeletal shadows across the dusty floor. Taking a deep breath, Moe shouldered his backpack, the weight of their makeshift tools - a crowbar and a silenced pistol - a heavy burden. With a final glance at Sarah and Celia, he slipped out of the ranger station, melting into the pre-dawn darkness.

The trek towards the mine was a nerve-wracking affair. Using the blueprints Sarah had obtained, Moe navigated a labyrinth of overgrown paths and abandoned mining equipment. The oppressive silence was broken only by the occasional screech of an owl or the distant growl of a guard dog.

Finally, he reached the ventilation shaft, a rusted metal contraption spewing stale air from the mine's depths. Carefully, using the crowbar, he pried

open the access panel, the screech of
metal on metal a jarring sound in the
quiet morning.   Peering into the
darkness, he could see a narrow metal
ladder disappearing into the inky abyss.
Taking another deep breath, he lowered
himself into the shaft, the rusty rungs
groaning under his weight. The air grew
thick and stale, the darkness absolute.
He relied solely on his sense of touch,
his heart pounding a frantic rhythm
against his ribs.

After what felt like an eternity, his
feet touched solid ground.   He found
himself in a cramped tunnel, lit only by
the faint glow of his flashlight. The
air was thick with the smell of dust and
sweat, an oppressive silence broken only
by the distant drip of water.

Following the faint sound of voices, he
navigated the labyrinthine tunnels, his
senses on high alert.   Finally, he

emerged into a vast cavern, a scene straight out of a dystopian nightmare. Dim lights cast an eerie glow on rows upon rows of skeletal figures hunched over pickaxes, their faces obscured by sweat and grime. The air hung heavy with the rhythmic clanging of metal on rock, a symphony of human misery.

A sense of overwhelming nausea washed over Moe. These weren't miners, they were prisoners, driven to their knees by exhaustion and fear. He spotted his source, a wiry man with haunted eyes and a tremor in his hands, frantically shoveling ore into a rusted cart.

He made eye contact with Moe, a flicker of recognition followed by a look of panicked terror. Before the source could react, a burly guard with a cruel sneer lumbered towards them. He barked an order in a language Moe didn't understand, but the menacing glint in his eyes needed no translation.

Thinking fast, Moe grabbed the source and shoved him back into the line of workers. The guard, surprised by the sudden movement, reached for his baton. Adrenaline surged through Moe's veins. He lunged forward, grabbing the guard's wrist and twisting it with a practiced flick.

The guard howled in pain, dropping his baton. Moe followed up with a swift knee to the groin, sending the guard crumpling to the cavern floor. The noise echoed through the vast chamber, momentarily breaking the rhythm of work.

The other guards, alerted by the commotion, whirled around, their faces contorted in rage. But before they could react, a voice boomed through the cavern.

"What's the meaning of this?"

A tall, imposing figure emerged from the shadows, his face obscured by the dim light. He wore a pristine white suit, a stark contrast to the grimy environment, and exuded an aura of cold authority. This was no ordinary guard; this was the man in charge.

Moe, his heart hammering against his ribs, knew he was in over his head. He had to get the evidence and get out of there before all hell broke loose. He glanced towards the ventilation shaft, a sliver of daylight peeking through the opening high above.

"You!" the man in white barked, pointing a finger at Moe. "Explain yourself!"

Acting on instinct, Moe pointed the silenced pistol at the man in white. "This is just a misunderstanding," he said, his voice surprisingly steady despite the tremor in his hands. "I think I got lost on my hike."

The man in white's lips twisted into a sneer. "A hiker with a gun? I don't think so."

Suddenly, a high-pitched squeal pierced the air. A spotlight flickered to life, illuminating a figure rappelling down the ventilation shaft – Celia, her face a mask of determination. She landed gracefully beside Moe, the camera clutched tightly in her hand.

"Let's go!" Moe yelled, grabbing Celia's arm and dragging her towards the shaft.

A cacophony of shouts and angry curses erupted behind them. Guards descended upon them like a pack of wolves, batons raised and faces contorted in fury. Moe knew they wouldn't get out unscathed.

Just as they reached the shaft, a blow connected with Moe's shoulder, sending him sprawling. Celia screamed, her grip on the camera loosening. But before a guard could snatch it, Sarah materialized

from the darkness, a length of pipe clutched in her hand. She swung wildly, connecting with a guard's head with a sickening thud.

With a surge of adrenaline, Moe scrambled to his feet. He grabbed the dangling rope ladder and began to climb, pulling Celia with him. Bullets whizzed past them, spitting sparks from the metal rungs. They clambered up as fast as they could, Sarah providing them with cover fire from below.

Finally, they reached the top, collapsing onto the damp earth outside the ranger station. Sarah, bruised but breathing, followed them shortly after. They could hear the frustrated shouts of the guards echoing from the mine entrance, but they were safe, for now.

Celia, shaken but resolute, retrieved the camera. "We got it," she gasped, her voice trembling. "We got the evidence."

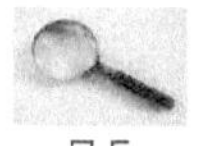

Moe looked at the small device, a symbol
of hope in their desperate fight. They
had walked into the lion's den and
emerged, battered but unbroken. Now, the
real fight would begin. They had the
proof, the incriminating footage of the
enslaved workers and the deplorable
conditions within the mine. It was time
to expose Horizon Resources and bring
them to justice, for Miguel, for the
innocent victims trapped beneath the
earth, and for themselves, the unlikely
heroes who dared to challenge a powerful
corporation.

As they watched the first rays of dawn
paint the sky in hues of orange and pink,
a sense of accomplishment mingled with
exhaustion settled over them. They had
achieved the impossible, infiltrated the
heavily guarded mine and secured the
evidence. But the true test was yet to
come.

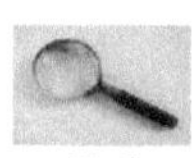

Back at Sarah's cluttered apartment, the air thick with stale coffee and nervous energy, they reviewed the footage captured by the camera. The grainy images, shaky at times due to their hasty escape, were nonetheless a damning indictment of Horizon Resources' crimes. Emaciated figures toiled under harsh conditions their faces etched with despair. The overwhelming evidence left no room for doubt - forced labor, environmental damage, and a blatant disregard for human life.

"This is gold," Sarah muttered, her eyes gleaming with a fierce determination. "This will blow the lid off this whole operation. But getting it out there, that's another story."

The media landscape was a minefield of its own. Mainstream outlets, beholden to corporate advertising dollars, were often hesitant to bite the hand that fed

them. They needed someone willing to take a risk, a journalist with a reputation for chasing the truth regardless of the consequences.

Their search led them to David Stern, a grizzled investigative reporter with a shock of white hair and a gaze that could pierce steel. Stern, known for his relentless pursuit of justice, had a long history of ruffling feathers in high places. He listened to their story his face grim as he watched the footage.

"This is big," Stern said, his voice gravelly. "This could be the story that breaks Horizon Resources wide open. But be warned, they don't play nice. They have lawyers, lobbyists, and enough money to bury this story deeper than you can imagine."

Moe understood the risks. They were already on Horizon Resources' radar, their faces likely plastered on security

footage circulating among private security firms. But backing down wasn't an option. They had a moral obligation to expose the truth, to give a voice to the voiceless victims trapped within the mine.

"We know the risks," Moe said, his voice firm. "But we can't just stand by and do nothing. These people deserve justice." Stern nodded, a flicker of respect in his eyes. "Alright," he said, a gruff smile playing on his lips. "Let's give them a story they won't forget. But we need to be smart about this. We can't just throw this out there and expect fireworks."

A plan began to take shape. Stern, with his network of contacts, would leak the footage anonymously to select media outlets, ones with a reputation for independent reporting. They would create a media storm, a wave of public outrage

that would force the authorities to take action.

The days that followed were a whirlwind of activity. News outlets across the city picked up the story, the grainy footage of the mine a stark indictment of Horizon Resources' practices. Public outcry grew louder by the day, protests erupted outside the corporation's headquarters, and calls for a government investigation intensified.

Horizon Resources, their carefully cultivated image shattered, scrambled into damage control mode. They issued press releases filled with empty platitudes, launched smear campaigns against Stern and his sources, and threatened lawsuits against anyone who dared question their practices.

But the tide had turned. With each passing day, the evidence mounted, more whistleblowers came forward, and the

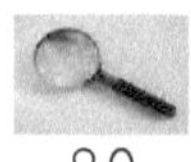

pressure on the authorities became undeniable. A federal investigation was launched, the mine was shut down, and arrest warrants were issued for the corporation's executives.

As the news of the investigation and arrests spread, a wave of relief washed over Moe, Sarah, and Celia. They had done it. They had exposed the truth and brought a powerful corporation to its knees. But their victory came at a cost. News of their involvement, leaked by a source within Horizon Resources with a grudge, made them targets. Death threats materialized, forcing them to move into safe houses, their lives forever changed. The shadow of fear became a constant companion, a stark reminder of the consequences of challenging powerful forces.

Yet, amidst the fear, there was a sense of pride. They had made a difference.

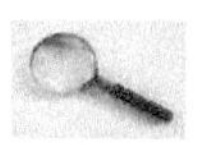

They had stood up for what was right and, in doing so, had inspired others to do the same. Miguel's death, though a tragedy, had not been in vain. His memory lived on, a beacon of courage and a testament to the power of ordinary people to fight for justice.

The midday sun beat down on Moe's back as he navigated the labyrinthine streets of Koreatown. Sweat beaded on his forehead despite the thin cotton t-shirt clinging to his well-worn frame. He wasn't used to this side of the city, the air thick with the aroma of kimchi and sizzling bulgogi wafting from open restaurant doors. He was here for a meeting, a blind date set up by his cousin, Marco, a boisterous Marine stationed overseas.

Moe finds a Partner

Marco, ever the matchmaker, had insisted Moe needed help with his fledgling PI business. The letter introduction was cryptic - "Turbo, a good kid, ex-military, wants to learn the ropes." Skepticism gnawed at Moe, but a part of him, the part yearning for a partner, a confidante in this clandestine world, couldn't ignore the possibility.

A beat-up Toyota Supra, its cherry red paint dulled by years of California sun, sat haphazardly parked in a narrow alley. Smoke curled from its hood, and a figure leaned against the fender, a cigarette dangling from their lips. As Moe approached, the figure straightened, revealing a young man, maybe mid-twenties, with a shaved head and a tattoo of a roaring tiger peeking out from beneath a worn t-shirt. This must be Turbo.

"Moe?" the man asked, his voice a gravelly rasp. He extinguished the cigarette with a flick of his wrist, the embers showering the asphalt.

"Yeah," Moe replied, extending a hand. "Marco's cousin."

Turbo's handshake was firm, his grip calloused. His eyes, a steely blue, held a guarded look, remnants of a past etched in their depths. "Turbo," he said simply.

"Nice ride," Moe commented, gesturing towards the Supra.

Turbo snorted. "More rust than ride these days. But Marco said you might have some work that needs muscle, not horsepower."

Moe studied him for a moment. There was a rawness in Turbo, a barely concealed intensity that resonated with him. He saw a reflection of his own past, the

84

restlessness that drove him towards this unconventional life after the Marines.

"Let's grab some coffee," Moe said, gesturing towards a nearby cafe. "Marco sings your praises, but everyone needs a good story."

Over steaming cups of strong coffee, Turbo unfolded his tale. He'd served in Afghanistan, seen his share of combat, and emerged with a Purple Heart and a restless spirit. Civilian life felt like a prison, the daily grind suffocating. Marco's mail, a lifeline thrown across the vast distance, had sparked a flicker of hope.

As Turbo spoke, a sense of kinship bloomed within Moe. He saw the echoes of his own struggles mirrored in this young man's eyes. The yearning for purpose, the need to channel the honed instincts and skills into something more than flipping burgers or guarding a mall entrance.

"Being a PI isn't all tailing cheating spouses and digging up dirt," Moe warned. "It can be dangerous, frustrating, and the paychecks ain't exactly fat."

Turbo leaned back in his chair, a wry smile playing on his lips. "Danger doesn't scare me, Mr. Reyes. And trust me, I can handle frustration. As for the pay, any job that beats staring at a cubicle wall is good enough for me."

A slow smile spread across Moe's face. He saw the glint of determination in Turbo's eyes, a spark that mirrored his own. Maybe, just maybe, Marco's matchmaking skills weren't so bad after all.

"Alright, Turbo," Moe said, his voice firm. "Let's see what you're made of. But first, a word of warning - this life

ain't for the faint of heart. You in or
out?"

Turbo stared back his expression
unreadable for a moment. Then, a slow
grin spread across his face, a glint of
excitement replacing the guarded look.
"Let's do this," he said, his voice
filled with a newfound resolve.

As they stepped out of the cafe, the
California sun beat down on them, casting
long shadows on the bustling street. A
new chapter unfolded before them, a
partnership forged in shared experiences
and a thirst for justice.

Miguel is Missing

The California sun beat down on Moe
"Snake-Eyes" Juarez's weathered face as
he slammed the creaky door of his office
shut. Inside, the air hung thick with the
scent of stale coffee and the nervous
sweat of his apprentice, Turbo. A young

kid, barely out of his teens, with a mop of jet-black hair and eyes that mirrored the chrome of a classic car.

"Alright, mijo," Snake-Eyes rasped, his voice worn thin from years of cigarettes and shouting over casino roars. "Looks like we got ourselves a hot one."

He tossed a crumpled photograph onto the desk. It showed a woman, her beauty marred by worry lines, clutching a faded picture of a smiling young man in a military uniform. "Dolores Rodriguez," Snake-Eyes explained. "Her son, Miguel, went missing two weeks ago. Fresh out of the Navy, stationed down at San Diego. Supposedly last seen at that new joint on Whittier Boulevard, The Purple Canary."

Turbo whistled. "The Canary? That's a hangout for some real shady characters. Gangsters, smugglers..."

"Exactly," Snake-Eyes nodded. "Dolores doesn't trust the cops. Says they ain't

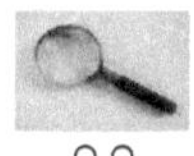

doing enough. She wants us to find Miguel."

The 1949 Ford Woody coughed and sputtered to life outside. Snake-Eyes, with Turbo in tow, navigated the sun-drenched streets of East LA. The Purple Canary, a garish neon sign perched on a rundown building, stood out like a sore thumb. Inside, the air was thick with cigarette smoke and the sounds of a mournful blues record. Men with greased hair and shifty eyes eyed them as they entered.

Snake-Eyes, a familiar face in the city's underbelly, approached a hulking man with a handlebar mustache guarding the bar. "Lefty," he greeted, the nickname dripping with irony. "Heard you might know something about a sailor named Miguel Rodriguez."

Lefty narrowed his eyes. "Don't know what you're talking about, Snake."

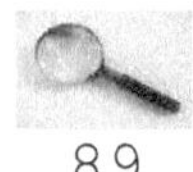

"Come on, Lefty," Turbo chimed in. "We both know this joint caters to more than just whiskey and dames."

Suddenly, a voice piped up from behind. "Looking for Miguel, huh?"

A wiry man, his face crisscrossed with wrinkles like a roadmap, emerged from the shadows. "He ain't here anymore," he continued, a sly grin playing on his lips. "But I know where he might be. For a price."

Snake-Eyes exchanged a glance with Turbo. The trail had gone hot, but the price of information in the underbelly of East LA was often measured in danger.

The smoky air hung heavy with unspoken threats as Snake-Eyes squared his shoulders. "Price, huh? What's your name, pops?"

"Call me Wink," the wizened man rasped, his voice gravelly like sandpaper. "And

the price for Miguel's whereabouts is simple. You gotta get me something."

He leaned closer, his breath reeking of stale beer and something stronger. "There's a shipment coming in for Big Louie down by the docks. You snag a package for me, I tell you where Miguel's headed."

Snake-Eyes' gut clenched. Big Louie was a notorious gangster, and interfering with his business was a guaranteed path to a bullet-riddled future. But Miguel's worried mother's face flashed in his mind.

"What's in the package?" Turbo blurted, his youthful naivete cutting through the tense atmosphere.

Wink chuckled, a dry, humorless sound. "That, mijo, ain't none of your concern." Snake-Eyes considered his options. The cops wouldn't touch a case involving Big Louie without a mountain of evidence, and

Dolores was desperate. He met Wink's gaze, a silent decision passing between them.

"Alright, Wink," Snake-Eyes finally said, his voice betraying none of the turmoil within. "We'll get you your package. But you better not be leading us on a wild goose chase."

A satisfied smirk spread across Wink's wrinkled face. "You won't regret this, Snake. Now, about that shipment..."

He launched into a detailed description of the operation, his words painting a picture of a bustling dock at midnight, guarded thugs, and a crate marked with a specific symbol. As Wink spoke, Snake-Eyes formulated a plan, his mind a steel trap snapping shut around the details. He knew this was a gamble, a dangerous game played in the shadows. But for Miguel, and for the sliver of hope in Dolores' eyes, he was willing to roll the dice.

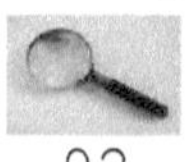

Later that night, under the cloak of a starless sky, Snake-Eyes and Turbo found themselves crouching behind a stack of crates on the bustling San Pedro docks. The salty tang of the ocean filled their nostrils, a stark contrast to the stale cigarette smoke of The Purple Canary. The air crackled with nervous anticipation.

"Remember the plan, Turbo?" Snake-Eyes murmured, his voice barely a whisper.

Turbo, his face grim, nodded. "Distraction, grab the package, and get out clean."

A low rumble echoed in the distance, growing louder until a hulking freighter loomed into view. Activity surged on the docks as burly men in overalls unloaded cargo. Snake-Eyes pointed to a group of figures huddled near a crate marked with the symbol Wink described.

"That's them," he hissed.

Turbo took a deep breath, his bravado replaced by a steely resolve. Snake-Eyes clapped him on the shoulder, a silent reassurance in the darkness. Then, with a well-rehearsed yell, Turbo sprang out from their hiding place, drawing the attention of the dockworkers.

Chaos erupted. Shouts and curses filled the air as men scrambled for cover. Snake-Eyes seized the opportunity, darting towards the marked crate like a viper. He wrestled open the latch, adrenaline coursing through his veins. Inside, nestled amongst packing peanuts, lay a wrapped package.

Just as Snake-Eyes secured the package, a large hand clamped down on his shoulder. He whirled around to find himself face-to-face with a hulking thug, his eyes burning with rage.

"You made a big mistake, friend," the thug growled, his voice a low rumble.

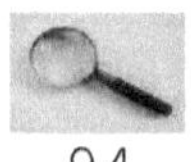

The thug's grip tightened like a vise, his knuckles turning white. Snake-Eyes, caught off guard, felt a surge of panic. He wasn't young anymore, the years spent chasing shadows and dodging fists taking their toll. But giving up wasn't an option. Not with Miguel's life potentially hanging in the balance.

With a burst of adrenaline, Snake-Eyes slammed his elbow into the thug's gut, eliciting a grunt of pain. The grip loosened momentarily, giving Snake-Eyes the precious window he needed. He whipped a roundhouse kick, catching the thug square in the chest. The impact sent the goon staggering back, momentarily stunned.

Turbo, ever the quick learner, seized the opportunity. He moved forward, a stray pipe wrench clutched in his hand. With a yell that surprised even himself, he connected with the side of the thug's

head. The wrench clanged as it met bone, and the thug crumpled to the ground, unconscious.

Snake-Eyes, his chest heaving, wasted no time. He shoved the package into his trench coat, a cold sweat prickling his skin. Shouts echoed from across the dock as the other thugs, alerted by the commotion, started converging towards them.

"Go!" Snake-Eyes barked at Turbo, already sprinting towards the labyrinth of crates and cargo containers. They needed to disappear, fast.

Turbo, shaken but determined, followed close behind. They weaved through the maze, the metallic clang of containers and the shouts of approaching thugs a terrifying symphony. Snake-Eyes' lungs burned with each desperate breath, his old bones protesting the exertion.

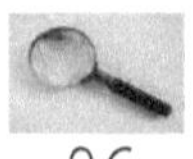

Suddenly, a dead end. A towering wall of containers blocked their path. Snake-Eyes cursed under his breath. They were trapped.

"Up!" Turbo yelled, pointing towards a precarious stack of crates barely clinging to life. It was their only option.

Snake-Eyes, ever the pragmatist, knew the climb was risky. One wrong move and they'd be crushed beneath the toppling crates. But the alternative was far worse. He gritted his teeth and started climbing, the rough wood digging into his palms.

Turbo followed close behind, his youthful agility making him ascend with surprising ease. Just as they reached the top, the shouts of the thugs reached a crescendo. They were close.

Snake-Eyes peered over the edge. Below, a forklift rumbled towards them, its

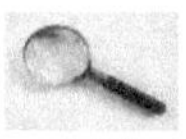

driver oblivious to the drama unfolding above. An idea, desperate but potentially their only escape, sparked in his mind. "Hold on!" he yelled at Turbo, grabbing a loose chain dangling from a nearby container.

With a strength born of desperation, Snake-Eyes swung the chain, aiming for the forklift's windshield. It connected with a resounding crack, shattering the glass and sending the startled driver swerving. The forklift lurched, narrowly missing a stack of crates, and came to a halt, its engine sputtering in protest. The commotion bought them precious seconds. Using the chain as a makeshift anchor, Snake-Eyes rappelled down the side of the container stack, landing with a thud on a pile of discarded burlap sacks. Turbo followed suit, landing with a yelp of pain that was fortunately

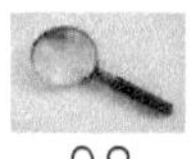

drowned out by the irate shouts of the approaching thugs.

They scrambled to their feet, adrenaline masking the throbbing pain in their limbs. They had to get out of there, and fast.

Snake-eyes spotted a narrow alleyway between two towering warehouses, barely wide enough for a single person. It was a tight squeeze, but their only hope.

"This way!" he yelled, shoving Turbo through the opening. He followed suit, the rough brick scraping against his back.

They emerged on the other side of the alley, coughing and gasping for breath. The shouts of the thugs had faded into the distance. For a moment, they simply stood there, leaning against the cold brick wall, their chests heaving with exertion.

"We...we made it," Turbo panted, a shaky smile spreading across his face.

Snake-Eyes nodded, a wave of relief washing over him. They were battered and bruised, but alive. And most importantly, they had the package.

"Now the real question," Snake-Eyes rasped, his voice hoarse. "What the hell is in this thing?"

Carefully, he unwrapped the package, revealing a small, ornately carved wooden box. Intricate symbols, alien to Snake-Eyes' eyes, were etched onto the surface. As he lifted the lid, a soft, blue light emanated from within.

Inside, nestled in velvet lining, lay a single, perfect sapphire. It pulsed with an otherworldly glow, casting an ethereal light on their faces. Snake-Eyes had never seen anything like it.

But one thing was certain - this wasn't just some smuggled jewel. This sapphire

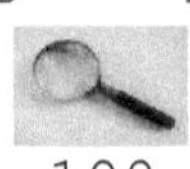

held a secret, one far more dangerous than they could have ever imagined.

The sapphire pulsed in Snake-Eyes' hand, its captivating blue light contrasting starkly with the grimy reality of the dockyard alley. A shiver ran down his spine, not just from the cool night air but from a sense of unease that settled deep in his gut. This wasn't just a simple smuggling operation gone wrong. This sapphire, with its otherworldly glow, was something more.

"What do you think it is?" Turbo whispered, his voice barely audible over the pounding of his own heart. The sapphire seemed to draw him in, a hypnotic beacon in the darkness.

Snake-Eyes shook his head, his weathered face etched with concern. "Beats me, kid. But one thing's for sure, it ain't worth risking our lives over."

He re-wrapped the box and tucked it deep inside his trench coat. The weight of it felt far greater than its size. They needed to get back to the office, regroup, and figure out what they'd stumbled into.

The journey back was silent, a stark contrast to the adrenaline-fueled escape. The city lights seemed to shimmer with a strange luminescence, reflecting the sapphire's unsettling glow beneath Snake-Eyes' coat.

Back at the office, the stale scent of cigarettes and dust offered a strange sense of familiarity. Snake-Eyes switched on the lone desk lamp, casting a pool of harsh yellow light on the worn wooden table.

He placed the wrapped box on the desk, its presence filling the small room with an oppressive silence. Turbo, ever

impulsive, reached out a hand to touch it.

"Don't," Snake-Eyes snapped, his voice sharp. "Whatever it is, it's dangerous." Turbo flinched his bravado momentarily subdued. Shamefaced, he withdrew his hand.

"We need to find Wink," Snake-Eyes continued, his mind already formulating a plan. "He might know what this thing is, and where it came from."

But finding Wink wouldn't be easy. The man was a ghost in the city's underbelly, appearing and disappearing like smoke on the wind.

"Maybe we can use Dolores," Turbo suggested. "She might know someone who could point us in the right direction." Snake-Eyes considered this. Dolores, desperate to find her son, might be willing to make deals with anyone who

offered a lead. But the risk of involving her in this dangerous game was high.

"We'll cross that bridge when we come to it," Snake-Eyes finally said. "For now, let's get some rest. We'll need all our strength for what's coming next."

The night stretched on, filled with the restless tossing and turning of troubled sleep. The sapphire pulsed beneath Snake-Eyes' coat, a constant reminder of the mystery they were entangled in. As dawn broke, casting a pale light through the dusty office window, he knew one thing for certain - their simple case of a missing sailor had become something far more sinister.

Their next steps were uncertain. They had the sapphire, a dangerous and possibly valuable object. They needed information, and Wink was their only lead. But approaching him would be perilous. Dolores, Miguel's mother,

could be a source of help, but bringing her into this web of danger felt wrong.

Snake-Eyes rose from his makeshift bed on the office couch, his muscles protesting the night's poor sleep. He looked at Turbo, who was still fast asleep, exhaustion etched on his young face. This case was bigger than either of them could have imagined. They were in over their heads, but backing out wasn't an option. The safety of Miguel, Dolores, and potentially the entire city might depend on them unraveling the secrets of the pulsating sapphire.

He brewed a strong pot of coffee, the bitter scent filling the office. As he took a sip, his mind raced. They needed a plan, a way to navigate this murky water without getting pulled under. He needed to contact his old friend, Miguel "El Halcón" (The Falcon) Rodriguez, a former con artist with connections to all

corners of the city's underworld. El
Halcón might be just the person they
needed to find Wink and unravel the
mystery of the sapphire. But reaching out
to El Halcón meant venturing back into a
past Snake-Eyes had tried to leave
behind, a past filled with danger and
regret.

The morning sun climbed higher, casting
its harsh light on the dusty office.
Snake-Eyes knew he had a decision to
make. He could walk away, leave the
sapphire and the mystery behind. But
something in his gut, the same instinct
that had kept him alive all these years,
told him he couldn't. He had a
responsibility to Miguel, to Dolores, and
to the city itself. He had to see this
through, no matter the cost.

The decision weighed heavily on Snake-
Eyes as he stared into the lukewarm
coffee in his mug. Reaching for El Halcón

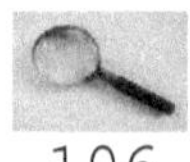

was a gamble, a dance with the devil he'd sworn off years ago. But the alternative - leaving Dolores hanging and Miguel potentially trapped in some web of intrigue - was even more unpalatable.

With a resigned sigh, Snake-Eyes retrieved a crumpled photograph from a drawer. It showed a younger, sharper-dressed version of himself alongside a grinning man with a mischievous glint in his eyes. That was El Halcón, a man who could navigate the city's underbelly like a fish in a river, his network of contacts stretching from petty thieves to high-rolling gangsters.

"Alright, El Halcón it is," Snake-Eyes muttered, a flicker of steel returning to his eyes. He knew the risks - El Halcón wouldn't deal in favors, only in leverage. But Snake-Eyes had a chip to bargain with now - the sapphire.

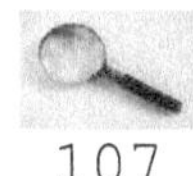

Finding El Halcón wouldn't be easy. He rarely stayed in one place for long, flitting from one shady joint to another like a phantom. But Snake-Eyes knew his haunts - a smoky jazz club called "The Blue Note," a greasy spoon diner frequented by crooked cops, and a seedy gambling den known as "The Lucky Ace."

He decided to start with The Blue Note. The smoky haze hung thick in the air as Snake-Eyes entered, the mournful melody of a saxophone weaving through the chatter and clatter of glasses. His eyes scanned the dimly lit room, searching for a familiar face.

A weathered barkeep with a handlebar mustache noticed him. "Looking for someone, friend?" he rasped, his voice raspy from years of inhaling secondhand smoke.

"El Halcón," Snake-Eyes answered, keeping his voice low.

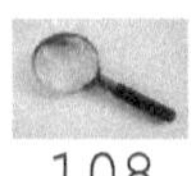

The barkeep raised an eyebrow, a flicker of recognition crossing his face. "He ain't a regular here, but I might know where he might be tonight. You got something for him?"

Snake-Eyes nodded, tapping his coat pocket where the sapphire lay hidden. The barkeep's grin widened, a glint of avarice flashing in his eyes.

"Alright, here's the deal," he said, leaning in conspiratorially. "He'll be at The Lucky Ace after midnight. But he only deals with those who come bearing gifts."

Snake-Eyes knew the barkeep was likely trying to cut himself a piece of the action. He tossed a couple of crumpled bills on the counter. "Consider it your finder's fee. And keep my visit a secret."

The barkeep's smile widened as he pocketed the money. "Your lips are

sealed, friend. Now, how about a drink to celebrate your… good fortune?"

Snake-Eyes declined, a knot of unease tightening in his gut. El Halcón's presence at The Lucky Ace, a notorious den of violence and vice, didn't bode well. This wasn't just about finding Wink anymore; it was about navigating a web of danger that threatened to swallow them whole.

The rest of the day was a blur. Snake-Eyes prepped Turbo, explaining the risks involved in approaching El Halcón. He warned him to stay hidden while he did the talking. As night fell, a sense of foreboding settled over them.

The Lucky Ace was everything Snake-Eyes remembered and more. Dimly lit with flickering bulbs, the air crackled with tension and the stench of stale beer. Gruff men with shifty eyes huddled around greasy tables, cards flashing in the dim

light. A haze of cigarette smoke hung heavy in the air, punctuated by the occasional raucous laugh or guttural curse.

Snake-Eyes spotted El Halcón at a back table, surrounded by a group of burly thugs. The years hadn't been kind to him. Lines etched his face, and his once-bright eyes now held a cynical glint. Yet, his posture remained confident, a predator surveying his territory.

Snake-Eyes took a deep breath and approached the table, Turbo trailing nervously behind. The thugs shifted, their eyes narrowing as the newcomers approached. El Halcón looked up, a flicker of recognition crossing his face as his gaze met Snake-Eyes'.

"Snake-Eyes," he drawled, his voice smooth as silk but laced with underlying threat. "Been a long time. To what do I owe the pleasure?"

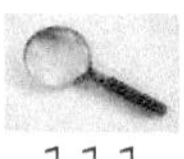

"We need your help," Snake-Eyes replied, his voice steady despite the churning in his gut. He reached into his pocket, his hand brushing against the cool surface of the sapphire. "We have something… something you might be interested in."
El Halcón's gaze followed the movement, a hint of curiosity replacing the initial animosity. He gestured for a seat at the table, his thugs parting to let them pass. Snake-Eyes and Turbo sat down,
The air crackled with tension as Snake-Eyes slid into the worn leather booth across from El Halcón. The thugs flanking the conman barely glanced at Turbo, their beady eyes fixated on Snake-Eyes, their hands hovering near concealed weapons. El Halcón leaned back, a sardonic smile playing on his lips.

"Let's hear it then, Snake-Eyes," he drawled, his voice laced with amusement. "What kind of trouble have you stumbled

into that requires the services of El Halcón?"

Snake-Eyes met his gaze squarely. "We're looking for a man named Wink," he explained, his voice low and measured. "He might have information about a… situation we're involved in."

El Halcón's smile vanished, replaced by a flicker of suspicion. "Wink? You don't just stumble upon information about Wink. What's in it for you?"

Taking a deep breath, Snake-Eyes reached into his pocket, his fingers brushing against the cool, pulsing sapphire. He carefully placed it on the table, the gem's otherworldly glow illuminating the faces around him. A collective gasp rippled through the room.

El Halcón's eyes widened in surprise. He leaned closer, his gaze locked on the sapphire. "Where did you get this?" he

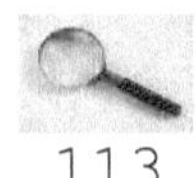

rasped his voice devoid of its usual flippancy.

"Long story," Snake-Eyes replied, his hand hovering over the gem. "Let's just say it's… complicated. We need to know what it is and where it came from. And Wink might have the answers."

El Halcón studied the sapphire, his brow furrowed in thought. The silence stretched, thick with unspoken questions. Finally, he spoke, his voice barely a whisper.

"This sapphire," he began, his voice laced with awe. "It's called the Eye of Ra. Legend says it belonged to an ancient Egyptian pharaoh, imbued with untold power."

A sense of dread settled in Snake-Eyes' stomach. He'd stumbled upon something far bigger than a missing sailor or a smuggled jewel. This sapphire, the Eye of

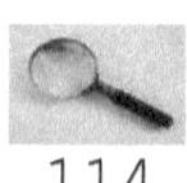

Ra, held a power that could potentially be used for unimaginable purposes.

"And Wink?" Turbo blurted out, unable to contain his curiosity any longer.

El Halcón's gaze snapped towards the young man, a dangerous glint in his eyes. "Wink," he said, his voice low and menacing, "knows more about the Eye of Ra than anyone else in this city. But he doesn't talk easily. He'll need convincing."

"What kind of convincing?" Snake-Eyes asked, a steely resolve hardening his gaze.

El Halcón chuckled, a cold, humorless sound. "That, my friend," he said, his eyes gleaming with a hint of mischief, "is where things get interesting."

He leaned in closer, his voice dropping to a conspiratorial whisper. "There's a shipment coming in tomorrow night. A shipment that Wink has his eye on. Help

me secure it, and I'll guarantee you a meeting with him. But be warned," he added, his voice hardening, "this won't be a walk in the park."

Snake-Eyes locked eyes with El Halcón, a storm brewing behind his weathered face. He knew this was a dangerous proposition. El Halcón was a snake, and this deal reeked of a double-cross. But with Miguel's life potentially hanging in the balance, he had no choice.

"Alright," Snake-Eyes finally said, his voice firm. "We'll help you with your shipment. But you better hold up your end of the bargain."

A grin stretched across El Halcón's face, revealing a gold tooth that glinted in the dim light. "Excellent," he said, clapping his hands together. "Now, let's get you boys a drink. You're going to need it for what lies ahead."

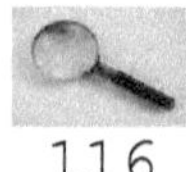

As Snake-Eyes and Turbo nursed their drinks, a knot of unease tightened in their stomachs. They had just made a deal with the devil, and the price might be far higher than they could have ever imagined. The quest to find Miguel and unravel the mystery of the Eye of Ra had taken a perilous turn, and they were hurtling towards a dangerous encounter that could change their lives forever.

The stale beer burned in Snake-Eyes' throat, a poor substitute for the churning of his gut. He and Turbo sat amidst El Halcón's entourage, the air thick with the stench of sweat, stale smoke, and a barely veiled threat. The smoky haze obscured faces, adding to the sense of unease gnawing at him.

"The shipment comes in at the abandoned steel mill on the outskirts," El Halcón continued, his voice low and smooth. "It

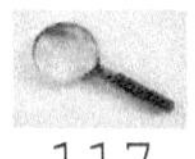

arrives by midnight, heavily guarded. Get it in, get out, and Wink's all yours."

Snake-Eyes raised an eyebrow. "That sounds too easy, El Halcón. What's the catch?"

El Halcón's lips twisted into a smirk. "Always the skeptic, Snake-Eyes. The catch is this - you're not dealing with amateurs here. This crew is ruthless, and they won't hesitate to kill anyone who gets in their way."

He glanced at Turbo, a predatory glint in his eyes. "Especially the inexperienced ones."

Turbo's eagerness was momentarily overshadowed by the weight of El Halcón's words. Snake-Eyes placed a reassuring hand on his shoulder, a silent message of calm amidst the storm.

"We can handle it," Snake-Eyes said, his voice firm despite the trepidation

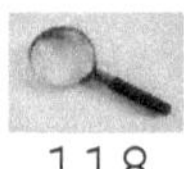

118

gnawing at him. "Just tell us the details."

El Halcón launched into a detailed explanation. The abandoned steel mill, a hulking skeleton casting a long shadow over the desolate landscape, was a known smuggling hub. The guards were ex-military, armed and dangerous. Their objective - a specific crate containing something valuable enough to warrant such high-level security.

As El Halcón spoke, Snake-Eyes formulated a plan. A desperate, risky plan, but their only option. They would need a diversion, a way to create chaos and snatch the crate amidst the confusion. He glanced at Turbo, a silent communication passing between them.

"We'll need a distraction," Snake-Eyes interrupted. "Something big enough to draw their attention away from the crate."

El Halcón chuckled, a cold, metallic sound. "Leave that to me, friend. I have a few… associates who enjoy a good fireworks display."

The rest of the night was spent in a tense, hurried preparation. El Halcón provided limited weaponry – a worn revolver for Snake-Eyes, a switchblade for Turbo. They weren't facing a war, El Halcón assured them, just a controlled chaos. But Snake-Eyes knew the line between controlled and chaotic could blur in the blink of an eye.

As the night deepened, they piled into El Halcón's beat-up jalopy, the rusted frame groaning under the unexpected weight. The car sputtered and coughed its way through the deserted streets, finally reaching the outskirts of the city where the skeletal silhouette of the abandoned steel mill loomed against the star-dusted night sky.

The air hung heavy with the smell of rust and decay. Eerie silence blanketed the place, broken only by the occasional screech of an owl or the rustle of unseen creatures in the tall grass. El Halcón dropped them off at a discreet distance, a mischievous glint in his eyes.

"Remember," he said, his voice a low rasp, "get the crate, find Wink, and get out. Don't become heroes, just shadows." With a final nod, he disappeared back into the darkness, leaving Snake-Eyes and Turbo under the inky cloak of the night. Snake-Eyes felt a pang of doubt. Had they just made a deal with the devil himself? But the thought of Miguel, of Dolores' worried face, spurred him into action.

They crept towards the abandoned mill, shadows flitting amongst the skeletal remains of machinery. The silence was deafening, broken only by the pounding of their hearts and the crunch of gravel

underfoot. Reaching the perimeter, they found a weak spot in the fence, a gap large enough for them to squeeze through. Inside the cavernous mill, darkness reigned supreme. The air, thick with dust and the metallic tang of rust, scratched their throats. They moved with practiced caution, using the shadows as their cloak. In the distance, they spotted a flicker of movement - the guards, heavily armed and patrolling the perimeter with a practiced vigilance.

Suddenly, a blinding flash illuminated the night sky, followed by a deafening boom that echoed through the mill, shaking the very foundations. It was El Halcón's distraction - a well-placed firework that had exploded near the entrance, drawing the guards' attention away from the other side of the building. This was their chance. Snake-Eyes and Turbo sprinted towards the center of the

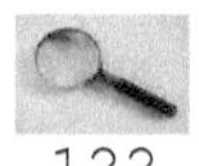

mill, their hearts pounding against their ribs. A single, large crate lay amidst a pile of crates, bathed in the harsh glow of a solitary hanging bulb.

As they neared, a guttural growl ripped through the air. Snake-Eyes whipped around, heart hammering against his ribs, to see a hulking figure emerge from the shadows. A man, built like a brick wall with a shaved head and a vicious scar running down his cheek, stood between them and the crate. He was no guard - this was muscle, hired muscle to ensure the operation ran smoothly.

"Looks like the party's getting crowded," the man snarled, his voice a gravelly rasp. He hefted a massive crowbar in his hand, the moonlight glinting off the cold steel.

Snake-Eyes drew his .38, the weight of the weapon an unfamiliar burden in his hand. He'd hoped to avoid a

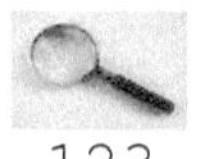

confrontation, but the situation had escalated beyond his control.

Turbo, ever impulsive, brandished his switchblade, despite the fear flickering in his eyes.

"Don't make me do this," Snake-Eyes rasped, hoping to buy some time. "We just want the crate, and then we'll be gone."

The man laughed, a harsh, humorless sound. "Nice try, old timer. This ain't a grocery store."

He fell forward, the crowbar whistling through the air. Snake-Eyes rolled to the side, narrowly avoiding the crushing blow. Turbo, caught off guard, stumbled back, the switchblade clattering to the dusty floor.

The ensuing chaos was a blur of movement and desperate struggle. Snake-Eyes fired a single shot, the deafening crack echoing in the vast chamber. The bullet ricocheted off a nearby pipe, showering

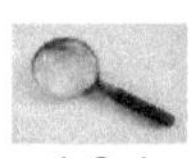

them with sparks. The goon roared, moving forward with renewed ferocity.

Snake-Eyes kicked a stray toolbox in his direction, tripping the man up momentarily. He scrambled to his feet, rage contorting his face. Just as the crowbar swung down towards him, a figure materialized from the shadows.

El Halcón, a wicked grin plastered on his face, held a wickedly curved knife to the goon's throat. The knife glinted in the moonlight, a silent threat.

"Party crasher, am I?" El Halcón drawled, his voice laced with amusement.

The goon's eyes widened in surprise. He glanced at the crate, then back at El Halcón, a flicker of recognition replacing the rage.

"El Halcón," he growled, the name sounding like a curse. "What are you doing here?"

El Halcón shrugged, his grin widening.
"Just taking care of some… unfinished
business. Now, why don't you take a
little vacation, hm?"
The goon hesitated, clearly recognizing
the advantage El Halcón held. With a
final menacing glare at Snake-Eyes and
Turbo, he backed away, disappearing into
the labyrinth of shadows within the mill.
Snake-Eyes and Turbo exchanged
bewildered glances. El Halcón's sudden
intervention had saved them from a brutal
encounter. But the question remained –
was this a genuine act of assistance, or
was there a deeper motive at play?
El Halcón sauntered towards the crate,
his movements fluid and predatory. "Well,
well," he murmured, kneeling before it.
"Looks like we got ourselves a prize."
He pried open the crate with a grunt,
revealing not a single package, but a
jumble of dusty artifacts – weathered

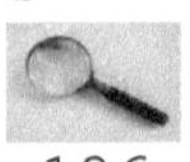

statues, tarnished amulets, and a crumbling scroll tied with a faded red ribbon. Disappointment washed over Snake-Eyes. The promised crate, the one containing their answer to Miguel and the Eye of Ra, was gone.

"What the…?" Turbo stammered his voice laced with confusion. "This isn't what we were looking for."

El Halcón rose, a frustrated snarl twisting his features. "Seems you got some bad intel, Snake-Eyes. This shipment's not what we expected."

He kicked a chipped clay figurine, sending it clattering across the dusty floor. Snake-Eyes felt a surge of anger. They had risked their lives, nearly gotten themselves killed, and for what? A crate full of worthless junk?

"You lied to us!" he roared, his voice echoing in the cavernous hall.

El Halcón met his gaze, his eyes cold and calculating. "Perhaps I did, Snake-Eyes. But sometimes, the best plans go awry." A tense silence descended upon them, broken only by the ragged gasps of their breaths. Snake-Eyes knew El Halcón was playing them, but for what purpose remained unclear. And most importantly, where was the real crate, the one containing the sapphire and potentially the key to finding Miguel?

Just then, a guttural growl ripped through the silence once more. The goon, seemingly emboldened by their distraction, reappeared in the doorway, a wicked grin plastered on his scarred face. He wasn't alone.

Three hulking figures flanked the goon, their faces obscured by shadow but their menacing presence unmistakable. Each man held a length of pipe, their eyes

gleaming with malicious intent. They had been outsmarted, ambushed.

El Halcón's playful demeanor vanished, replaced by a mask of steely resolve. "Looks like the party's getting bigger," he muttered, his voice devoid of its usual amusement.

Snake-Eyes cursed under his breath. They were outnumbered, outgunned, and cornered in the vast, echoing chamber. Panic threatened to rise, but he swiftly pushed it down. He needed to act, and fast.

"Turbo," he hissed, his voice barely audible over the pounding of his own heart. "Stick close and follow my lead." Turbo, his face pale but his gaze unwavering, nodded curtly. The switchblade lay forgotten on the dusty floor, useless against the brutal force they were about to face.

Snake-Eyes raised his revolver, a single shot left in the chamber. It was a desperate gamble, but it was their only chance. He aimed for a nearby pipe, hoping to create a distraction.

With a deafening crack, the bullet connected, showering them with a spray of sparks and dust. The goons flinched momentarily, startled by the unexpected sound. In that split second, Snake-Eyes lunged towards the crate, hoping to use it as cover.

The goon with the scar roared in rage, stepped forward with his pipe raised high. Snake-Eyes rolled to the side just as the pipe whistled through the air, missing him by a hair's breadth. He scrambled to his feet, the adrenaline coursing through his veins momentarily masking the ache in his aging bones.

Turbo, displaying surprising agility, snatched a rusty metal pipe from a nearby

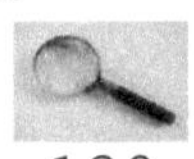

pile of debris. He met the charge of one of the other goons head-on, the clang of metal on metal echoing through the chamber. The fight was a brutal ballet of desperation, a struggle for survival in the heart of the abandoned steel mill. Snake-Eyes, his movements fueled by years of experience in the city's underbelly, engaged the scarred goon in a fierce duel. The goon was younger, stronger, but Snake-Eyes fought with the cunning of a cornered animal. He parried blows, used his agility to his advantage, and landed a few solid punches that sent the goon staggering back.

Just as Snake-Eyes thought he might gain the upper hand a deafening roar shattered the air. El Halcón, using a discarded crate as a makeshift shield, charged into the fray. His curved knife flashed in the dim light as he deflected a pipe blow aimed at him.

The battle intensified, the cavernous hall filled with the grunts of exertion, the clang of metal on metal, and the occasional yelp of pain. Snake-Eyes fought with a renewed sense of purpose, fueled by the desperate need to protect himself, Turbo, and the secrets potentially hidden within the abandoned mill.

The fight seemed to stretch on for an eternity, each second an agonizing test of their strength and resolve. One by one, the goons fell. The scarred goon, enraged by the beating he was taking from Snake-Eyes, fell forward with a reckless abandon. Snake-Eyes seized the opportunity, using a well-placed kick to send the man crashing into a pile of crates.

The goon lay there, groaning in pain, his pipe clattering away. With a ragged breath, Snake-Eyes turned his attention

to the remaining goon, who was now locked in a fierce struggle with El Halcón. Suddenly, a sickening crack echoed through the chamber. The goon clutched his arm, a look of horror spreading across his face. El Halcón, his eyes glinting with a cold fury, had plunged his knife deep into the goon's shoulder. The injured goon screamed, his grip loosening on his pipe. He stumbled back, before collapsing onto the dusty floor with a whimper. Silence descended upon the chamber, broken only by the ragged gasps of their breaths.

Snake-Eyes and El Halcón stood facing each other, both panting heavily, their bodies battered and bruised. A fragile truce hung in the air, the tension thick enough to cut with a knife.

"Seems we both underestimated the situation," El Halcón finally said, his voice raspy. He gestured towards the

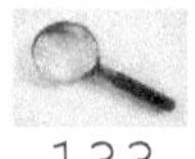

133

fallen goons with a bloody knife. "These weren't your average muscle for hire."
Snake-Eyes glared at him, suspicion gnawing at him. "Who were they then? And where's the real crate?"
El Halcón ran a hand through his sweat-slicked hair. "Looks like we both got played, Snake-Eyes. Someone knew about the shipment, someone who wanted that crate for themselves."
El Halcón limped towards the fallen goon with the scarred face, his eyes gleaming with a predatory glint. He knelt beside the unconscious man, his voice dripping with a chilling calmness as he spoke.
"Tell me," He rasped, the tip of his knife hovering dangerously close to the goon's scarred cheek, "who sent you?"
The goon whimpered, his eyes fluttering open to reveal a flicker of fear. "W-We don't know no names," he stammered, his

voice slurred with pain. "Just a… a symbol. A hawk with an eye."

El Halcón's eyes narrowed. The Hawk. A notorious black-market arms dealer with a reputation for ruthlessness and a network that stretched across the city's criminal underworld. His involvement in this mess sent a shiver down Snake-Eyes' spine.

"The Hawk," El Halcón spat, his voice laced with venom. "That explains why the shipment wasn't what we expected."

He rose, his gaze landing on the scattered artifacts in the crate. "Someone tipped the Hawk off about a valuable shipment, one that likely had nothing to do with these dusty relics."

Snake-Eyes' frustration mounted. They were back to square one, with no lead on the real crate or Miguel. "So, what now?" he asked, his voice laced with a barely contained anger.

El Halcón surveyed the scene, his gaze cold and calculating. "We need to find a way to talk to the Hawk," he said, his voice barely a whisper. "But approaching him directly is a death wish. We need leverage."

He glanced at the unconscious goon, then back at Snake-Eyes. A slow, cunning smile spread across his face.

"You see, Snake-Eyes," he said, his voice laced with a hint of amusement, "we might not have found the crate we were looking for, but we stumbled upon something far more interesting."

He gestured towards the goon's belt, where a small pouch hung conspicuously. El Halcón unfastened it with a practiced hand, revealing a worn leather-bound journal tucked inside.

"This," he declared, a glint of triumph in his eyes, "might be the key to unraveling this whole mess."

Intrigued, Snake-Eyes approached El Halcón. He recognized the journal – a type used by smugglers to record their transactions, their contacts, and their secrets. With this, they had a potential roadmap into the Hawk's shady world, a way to find the missing crate and perhaps even Miguel.

But there was a catch. Examining the journal, Snake-Eyes realized it was written in a complex code, a cipher likely known only to the goons themselves. Deciphering it would be a time-consuming task, one that could take days, even weeks.

"We can't waste that kind of time," Turbo interjected, his voice echoing in the cavernous hall. "Miguel could be in serious danger."

El Halcón nodded in agreement. "He's right, Snake-Eyes. We need to act fast.

But we can't just barge into the Hawk's territory without a plan."

He suggested a two-pronged approach. Snake-Eyes and Turbo would disappear, find a safehouse to lay low and attempt to crack the code. Meanwhile, El Halcón would use his network of informants to gather intel on the Hawk's whereabouts, his movements, and anything related to the missing crate.

Snake-Eyes grimaced. Laying low wasn't exactly his forte, but he understood the logic. Their best bet was to use their unique skillsets to approach the problem from different angles.

With a curt nod, they agreed to the plan. El Halcón helped them patch up their wounds, the silence thick with an uneasy truce. As dawn painted the sky with streaks of pink and orange, they emerged from the steel mill, leaving behind a

scene of violence and unanswered questions.

El Halcón melted back into the shadows, his parting words echoing in Snake-Eyes' ears: "Stay hidden, Snake-Eyes. And be careful what secrets you uncover."

Snake-Eyes and Turbo found themselves in a desolate part of the city, a maze of abandoned warehouses and crumbling brick buildings. They found a boarded-up apartment building, its windows dark and cavernous. It wasn't ideal, but it would have to do.

Inside, the air hung thick with dust and the stench of neglect. They barricaded the door with whatever debris they could find, a flimsy defense against any determined attacker. The journal lay open on a dusty table, its cryptic symbols mocking them.

Turbo, ever the optimist, tried a brute force approach, flipping through the

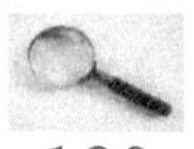

pages and attempting to decipher the patterns. But the code remained stubbornly inscrutable.

Snake-Eyes, known for his resourcefulness, rummaged through his meager supplies, a glint of determination in his steely gaze. He emerged with a small, weathered notebook - a relic from a bygone mission, filled with field notes and forgotten intel. Tucked within a pocket was a faded photograph, the edges frayed with time. It depicted a young woman, her eyes sparkling with mischief, a familiar warmth radiating from the image. Scarlett.

A spark ignited in his mind. Scarlett, with her vast knowledge and network of contacts, might hold the key to cracking the code. But contacting her meant putting her at risk. He hesitated, the image of his former teammate warring with his desperate need to find Miguel.

Turbo, sensing his internal struggle, placed a calloused hand on his shoulder. "We can't do this alone, Snake-Eyes," he said, his voice firm yet laced with understanding.

Snake-Eyes knew Turbo was right. He swallowed his anxieties, a silent promise forming in his gut. He wouldn't let Miguel or Scarlett down. With trembling fingers, he dialed a long-forgotten number, the burner phone feeling foreign in his hand.

The line crackled to life, a gruff voice answering on the other end. "Who is this?"

"It's me, Snake-Eyes," he rasped, his voice laden with years of unspoken stories.

A beat of startled silence followed, then a gasp. "Snake-Eyes? Is that really you?" It was Scarlett, her voice tinged with disbelief and a hint of something deeper.

Snake-Eyes explained their predicament, the cryptic journal, and the desperation gnawing at him. He spoke of Miguel's disappearance, the Hawk's involvement, and the looming threat.

Scarlett listened intently, a steely resolve hardening her voice. "Alright, Snake-Eyes," she said when he finished. "We'll figure this out. But contacting me was a risky move. Where are you?"

Snake-Eyes described their makeshift hideout, the tension in his chest tightening as he awaited her response.

After a moment, Scarlett spoke. "Stay put. I'll send someone to help you decipher the code. But this needs to be quick and clean. You can't stay off the grid for long."

Relief washed over Snake-Eyes, a wave of gratitude for his old friend. "Thank you, Scarlett," he said, his voice thick with emotion. "I owe you one."

"Don't worry about that," she replied, a hint of a smile in her voice. "Just keep Miguel safe. That's payment enough."

The call ended, leaving a fragile hope dangling in the air. Snake-Eyes relayed the message to Turbo, a flicker of optimism lighting up the young man's eyes. They settled down to wait, the silence punctuated only by the rhythmic ticking of a loose floorboard and the gnawing anxiety in their hearts.

Hours stretched into a tense vigil. The sun dipped below the horizon, painting the dusty windowpanes with hues of orange and purple. Just as despair threatened to creep in, a rhythmic pattern of taps sounded from the boarded-up window.

Snake-Eyes and Turbo exchanged a cautious glance. They inched towards the window, adrenaline coursing through their veins. With a swift movement, Snake-Eyes ripped away a section of the board, revealing a

slim, masked figure perched on the fire escape.

"Scarlett sent me," the figure rasped, their voice disguised with a voice modulator. "I'm here to help you crack the code."

Snake-Eyes and Turbo exchanged another look, a cautious welcome etched on their faces. This was their lifeline, their only chance to break through the cryptic puzzle and find Miguel. As the masked figure slipped inside, the night deepened, filled with the promise of a perilous journey into the heart of a criminal conspiracy.

The newcomer, shrouded in a dark cloak and a featureless mask, moved with practiced efficiency. They unfurled a worn leather satchel on the dusty table, its contents an eclectic mix of tools - magnifying glasses, codewheels, and stacks of worn reference books.

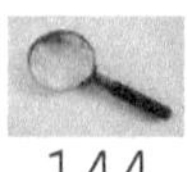

"The code appears to be a variant of a substitution cipher," the figure explained, their voice distorted by the modulator. "Each symbol likely represents a letter in the alphabet."
Snake-Eyes and Turbo leaned closer, their eyes scanning the pages of the journal, the cryptic symbols now appearing even more daunting under the harsh glare of a scavenged lamp. The newcomer, who introduced themself as Wraith, a trusted associate of Scarlett's, launched into a meticulous explanation.
"The key lies in identifying patterns," Wraith said, their voice a low murmur. "Look for recurring symbols, sequences that appear frequently. They might represent common words like 'the' or 'and'."
Hours melted into a blur of focused activity. Snake-Eyes, with his keen eye for detail, noticed a symbol consistently

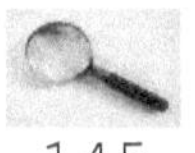

paired with another. He pointed it out,
and together they tested different letter
combinations, piecing together fragments
of words. Frustration mounted as progress
was slow, each breakthrough followed by
a string of dead ends.

Turbo, ever the optimist, kept the energy
high. He rummaged through the scavenged
supplies, finding a half-eaten bag of
stale chips and a dusty bottle of water.
He shared it with Snake-Eyes and Wraith,
the meager rations a reminder of their
precarious situation.

As the night wore on, the tension in the
air grew thicker. Every creak of the
floorboard sent shivers down their
spines. The city outside, usually a
symphony of honking horns and distant
sirens, seemed eerily silent.

Just as exhaustion threatened to
overwhelm them, a breakthrough arrived.

Wraith, hunched over a reference book, let out a triumphant cry.

"I found it!" they exclaimed, pointing to a specific symbol. "This one. It's a ligature, a combination of two letters used in older writing styles."

With renewed fervor, they cracked the code, deciphering symbol after symbol. The air crackled with anticipation as the fragmented words coalesced into legible sentences. The journal revealed a meticulous record of the Hawk's operations - smuggling routes, coded messages, and a list of aliases and safehouses.

But the most crucial piece of information was tucked away at the very back. A single sentence, written in larger, bolder script, sent a jolt of adrenaline through Snake-Eyes.

"Shipment secured. Eye of Ra transferred to Crimson Fist."

Crimson Fist. A notorious black-market auctioneer, known for dealing in high-value artifacts and stolen goods. The Eye of Ra had fallen into his clutches.

Snake-Eyes slammed his fist on the table, a surge of anger and determination coursing through him. He had to find Miguel, and he had to get the Eye of Ra back. But with the auction looming, time was running out.

"We need to contact Scarlett," he said, his voice tight with urgency. "She might know a way to infiltrate Crimson Fist's operation."

Wraith nodded their masked face unreadable. "I can set up a secure line. But be warned, Snake-Eyes. Crimson Fist is a dangerous man. Entering his auction is akin to walking into a viper's nest."

Snake-Eyes knew the risks, but he couldn't afford to back down. He took a deep breath, steeling himself for the

fight ahead. "We don't have a choice," he said, his gaze resolute. "Miguel and the Eye of Ra are depending on us."

With a newfound purpose, they contacted Scarlett. She confirmed their suspicions – Crimson Fist was holding an exclusive auction the following night, and the Eye of Ra was the prized possession.

The plan they formulated was audacious, bordering on suicidal. Snake-Eyes and Turbo would infiltrate the auction under assumed identities, hoping to locate Miguel and the Eye of Ra. Wraith, using their expertise in information gathering, would provide remote support and intel from a hidden location.

The night before the auction, adrenaline thrummed through their veins as they donned their disguises. Snake-Eyes, his weathered face hidden beneath a prosthetic beard and a fedora, transformed into a seasoned antiquities

dealer. Turbo, disguised as a youthful bodyguard, barely contained his nervous excitement.

With Scarlett's help, they procured forged identities and a hefty sum of black-market cash - their ticket into Crimson Fist's opulent den of iniquity. The air shimmered with anticipation as they stepped out of the shadows and into the heart of the unknown, ready to face the dangers that awaited them within the glittering walls of Crimson Fist's auction house.

The limousine glided through the city's underbelly, the flickering neon signs painting grotesque caricatures on Snake-Eyes' disguised face. Beside him, Turbo, his youthful features obscured by a carefully styled wig and a sharp suit, fidgeted with his collar, his apprehension barely concealed.

They were on their way to Crimson Fist's auction house, a sprawling art deco monstrosity that loomed over the decrepit skyline like a gaudy mausoleum. The air thrummed with a sinister energy, a mix of wealth, desperation, and veiled violence.

"Alright, here's the plan one last time," Snake-Eyes rasped, his voice distorted by the prosthetic beard. "We stick together, blend in, and keep our eyes peeled for Miguel and the Eye of Ra."

Turbo nodded curtly his eyes glued to the passing scenery. "What if things go south?" he whispered, his voice laced with a hint of fear.

"We improvise," Snake-Eyes replied, his voice firm despite the knot of worry twisting in his gut. "Just remember, our primary objective is finding Miguel. The Eye is secondary."

The limo pulled up to a velvet rope stretched taut across a red carpet. A pair of hulking bouncers, their faces etched with violence, scanned their forged invitations with practiced suspicion. Snake-Eyes, channeling his years of experience navigating the city's underbelly, exuded an air of quiet confidence.

He met their gaze with a practiced arrogance, his voice dripping with wealth when he spoke. "Mr. Durand and his associate," he announced, gesturing towards Turbo.

The bouncers grunted, their eyes lingering on the bulging briefcase clutched in Turbo's hand – a prop containing enough fake cash to buy their way into the auction. With a grudging nod, they were ushered past the velvet rope and into the opulent foyer.

The air inside was thick with the scent of expensive perfume and stale cigar smoke. Crystal chandeliers cast a garish glow on the marble floors and gilded statues. A motley crew of attendees milled about, their faces a mask of greed and avarice.

Snake-Eyes spotted a man in a flamboyant zoot suit, his fingers glittering with diamond rings, accosting a woman draped in enough jewels to rival a crown. A high-roller, one of Crimson Fist's loyal clientele. He nudged Turbo, discreetly pointing him out.

"Keep your eyes peeled for those types," he murmured. "They'll be our competition for the Eye."

As they navigated the throng, the booming voice of an auctioneer echoed from a grand hall at the far end. The auction had begun. Snake-Eyes quickened his pace, his heart hammering against his ribs.

Suddenly, a slender figure with fiery red hair materialized beside them. It was Wraith, their voice disguised through an earpiece. "Target identified," they hissed. "Miguel is being held in a secure room on the second floor, heavily guarded."

Snake-Eyes' blood ran cold. Miguel was alive, but imprisoned. They had to act fast. "We need a distraction," he muttered, his mind racing with possibilities.

Turbo, catching a glimpse of a serving tray laden with champagne flutes, grinned mischievously. With a well-placed bump, he sent the tray tumbling, shattering glasses and sending a cascade of bubbly liquid onto a group of high-society patrons.

Chaos erupted. Shrills of outrage filled the air as the drenched patrons sputtered and cursed. Snake-Eyes seized the

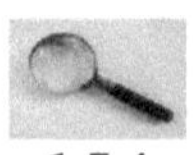

opportunity, grabbing Turbo's arm and leading him towards the staircase at the back of the hall.

The roar of the auction provided a convenient cover for their escape. They sprinted up the stairs, dodging startled guests and bewildered staff. Reaching the second floor, they found themselves in a dimly lit corridor, the air thick with dust and a faint metallic tang.

Cautiously, they crept down the hallway, their eyes scanning the numbered doors. A muffled groan from behind one doorway sent chills down Snake-Eyes' spine. It was Miguel.

With a silent nod, Snake-Eyes crouched before the door and pulled out a lockpicking kit he'd stashed in his pocket - a relic from his past life. His fingers danced across the pins, the rhythmic clicks a symphony to his ears.

The lock clicked open. Snake-Eyes threw the door open, his eyes adjusting to the dim light. Miguel, chained to a radiator, looked up, his face gaunt and bruised. Relief flooded Snake-Eyes.

"Miguel," he breathed, rushing to his side.

"Snake-Eyes?" Miguel stammered his voice raspy. "What are you doing here?"

Before Snake-Eyes could answer, a guttural growl ripped from the shadows. A hulking guard, alerted by the noise, stood menacingly in the doorway, his hand resting on the hilt of a wicked-looking dagger.

The guard's eyes narrowed, taking in the scene before him. Snake-Eyes, caught between freeing Miguel and facing the attack, cursed under his breath. Turbo, ever the quick thinker, seized the fallen champagne flute from his pocket.

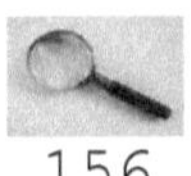

"Hey ugly!" he yelled, brandishing the shard of glass like a makeshift weapon. "Fancy a drink?"

The guard, momentarily distracted, scoffed at the challenge. But before he could react, Snake-Eyes sprang into action. Years of honed reflexes took over as he launched himself at the guard, aiming for a pressure point at the base of the neck.

A satisfying grunt escaped the guard's lips as he stumbled back, disoriented. Turbo, capitalizing on the opening, lunged forward and slammed the heavy door shut, throwing his weight against it to buy them precious seconds.

"Get the chains off him, Turbo!" Snake-Eyes barked, already scanning the room for another weapon. His eyes landed on a discarded metal pipe leaning against a dusty cabinet. Snagging it, he gripped it with a familiar fierceness.

Turbo wrestled with the rusty lock on the chain, his knuckles turning white with effort. Miguel, weak from his ordeal, slumped against the wall, his eyes wide with disbelief.

"Hurry, Turbo!" Snake-Eyes urged, his gaze glued to the straining door. It wouldn't hold for long.

Finally, with a satisfying snap, the lock yielded. Turbo shoved the chains aside, helping Miguel to his feet. The door creaked ominously, splintering under the guard's weight.

Snake-Eyes charged forward, swinging the pipe with all his might. The guard, regaining his senses, raised his dagger to parry the blow. Metal rang against metal, the echo echoing through the hallway.

The ensuing fight was brutal and fast-paced. Snake-Eyes, utilizing his years of hand-to-hand combat experience, fought

with a controlled ferocity, aiming for disarming blows rather than inflicting serious injury. Turbo, fueled by adrenaline, joined the fray, using his agility to harass the guard and create openings for Snake-Eyes.

The guard, though larger, was hampered by his bulky armor and the surprise attack. Miguel, fueled by a surge of renewed hope, joined the struggle, grabbing a metal chair and swinging it wildly.

The clash was a cacophony of shouts, grunts, and the clang of metal. Just as the guard seemed to gain the upper hand, a deafening roar shattered the air. The splintered door gave way, and a burly figure, presumably alerted by the commotion, charged into the room.

"What's the meaning of this racket?" the newcomer roared, his voice booming through the small space.

The guard, momentarily stunned, took a hesitant step back. This was their chance. With a final coordinated push, Snake-Eyes and Turbo shoved the guard aside, sending him crashing into the newcomer.

The two figures grappled on the floor, a tangled mess of limbs and curses. Seizing the opportunity, Snake-Eyes grabbed Miguel's arm and propelled him towards the opposite side of the room.

"Go!" he yelled his voice hoarse. "Find the Eye of Ra and get out of here!"

Confused but fueled by a primal instinct for survival, Miguel nodded curtly and bolted towards a side door he'd spotted earlier during the chaos. Just as he disappeared through the doorway, another group of guards, alerted by the commotion, rounded the corner and surged into the room.

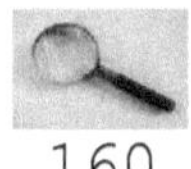

Snake-Eyes and Turbo, outnumbered and outmatched, braced themselves for another fight. But before they could react, a voice rang out from the staircase, clear and commanding.

"Hold your fire!"

It was Wraith, their masked savior, a pistol leveled at the approaching guards. They'd infiltrated the auction through the ventilation system and disabled the security cameras and created a diversion.

"We have hostages!" Wraith declared their voice amplified by a device hidden within their mask.

The guards hesitated, surprised by this unforeseen development. Snake-Eyes and Turbo took advantage of the confusion, melting behind Wraith and disappearing into the shadows behind the staircase.

A tense standoff ensued the air thick with hostility. The guards, unsure of the situation, opted to negotiate. With a

growl of frustration, they agreed to let Wraith and their "hostages" leave, unaware that their captives were the very people they were supposed to detain.

Emerging from the shadows, bruised but alive, Snake-Eyes and his companions raced through the dimly lit corridors, Miguel hot on their heels. The roar of the auction echoing through the building served as their guide, leading them towards their next objective - the Eye of Ra.

The frantic scramble through the opulent corridors was a blur. Adrenaline pumped through their veins each corner turned a potential ambush. Wraith, ever the tactician, barked instructions through their earpiece.

"Head south towards the exhibition hall," they directed. "According to the blueprints, the high-value items are stored there before the auction."

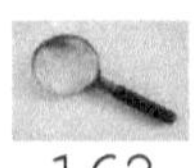

Snake-Eyes, his side throbbing from a blow received during the fight, helped Miguel along. The young man, though shaken, seemed surprisingly determined, his eyes burning with a newfound resolve. Just as they reached a grand set of double doors leading to the exhibition hall, a chilling announcement boomed through the hidden speakers.

"Attention all guests," a smooth, oily voice declared. "There has been a minor disturbance involving a security breach. Our security personnel are currently apprehending the perpetrators. The auction will resume shortly with a very special bonus item - the legendary Eye of Ra!"

Snake-Eyes cursed under his breath. Crimson Fist was playing his hand early, hoping to capitalize on the commotion they'd caused. They had to find the Eye before it went under the hammer.

Bursting through the double doors, they found themselves in a vast hall bathed in soft spotlights. Rows of glass display cases showcased priceless artifacts – jeweled daggers, intricately carved statues, and golden chalices. But their focus remained singular – the Eye of Ra. Turbo, his keen eyes scanning the room, spotted a section cordoned off with red velvet ropes. A single spotlight illuminated a pedestal upon which sat a velvet-covered box. This had to be it.

"There!" he exclaimed, pointing towards the display.

Snake-Eyes nodded grimly. But reaching it wouldn't be easy. Two heavily armed guards stood sentinel on either side of the cordoned area, their gazes sweeping the room with practiced vigilance.

Thinking fast, Snake-Eyes devised a plan. He relayed his strategy to his companions in hushed tones. Miguel, despite his

initial reluctance, agreed to play his part.

With a coordinated push, Snake-Eyes and Turbo created a diversion, causing a display case to topple and shatter on the opposite side of the hall. The guards, startled by the commotion, momentarily turned their attention away from the Eye of Ra.

Seizing the opportunity, Miguel darted forward, his desperate need to retrieve the artifact lending him uncharacteristic speed. He slipped beneath the velvet ropes, his heart pounding a frantic rhythm against his ribs.

One of the guards noticed Miguel's movement and roared in anger. He jumped forward, but Snake-Eyes was already there. With a well-placed kick, he sent the guard sprawling onto the floor.

The ensuing fight was a desperate struggle. Turbo, armed with a metal pipe snatched from a fallen display stand, fought with surprising ferocity. Wraith, their voice crackling over the earpiece, provided real-time updates on approaching guards and security measures.

Just as it seemed they might be overwhelmed, Miguel emerged from behind the velvet ropes, a triumphant glint in his eyes. He held aloft a small, intricately carved wooden box, its surface shimmering with an otherworldly light.

"I got it!" he yelled his voice choked with emotion. "The Eye of Ra!"

But their celebration was short-lived. The booming voice on the speakers announced the imminent start of the auction for the very item they held. More

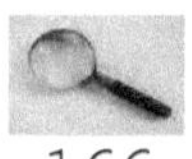

guards were converging on their location,
alerted by the commotion.

"We need to get out of here!" Wraith
urged their voice laced with urgency.
"There's a hidden exit near the back of
the hall. I can guide you."

With a final desperate glance at the
opulent surroundings, Snake-Eyes knew
they couldn't afford sentimentality. He
grabbed Miguel's arm and propelled him
towards the back of the hall, Turbo and
Wraith following close behind.

They weaved through a maze of exhibits,
adrenaline masking the fatigue creeping
into their limbs. Just as the first wave
of guards rounded the corner, they
reached a seemingly innocuous doorway
disguised as a bookcase.

Wraith, their fingers flying across a
hidden keypad, deactivated the security
lockdown. The bookcase swung open,

revealing a narrow passage bathed in cool darkness.

"This way!" Wraith barked, leading the charge into the unknown.

Behind them, the frustrated shouts of the guards echoed through the hall. Snake-Eyes, Miguel clutching the box containing the Eye of Ra tightly to his chest, followed Wraith into the darkness. The escape had just begun.

The passage was a cramped, dusty labyrinth that snaked its way through the bowels of the auction house. The stale air hung heavy with the scent of damp stone and forgotten memories. Wraith, their movements a blur in the dim light provided by a miniature headlamp, navigated the twists and turns with practiced ease.

"This maintenance tunnel leads to the building's underbelly," they explained over their earpiece, their voice a low

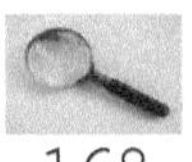

168

murmur. "It should eventually connect to the city's sewage system. Not the most pleasant escape route, but it'll get us out of Crimson Fist's clutches."

Snake-Eyes grunted in agreement. The thought of navigating a sewage tunnel wasn't appealing, but right now, survival trumped comfort. He focused on keeping Miguel close, the young man silent and surprisingly composed despite the ordeal.

The tunnel narrowed further, forcing them to hunch over, their progress becoming a slow, laborious crawl. The rhythmic drip of water echoed through the oppressive silence, punctuated by the occasional rustle of unseen creatures scuttling across the damp floor.

Just as claustrophobia threatened to overwhelm them, a faint glimmer of light flickered ahead. Hope surged through Snake-Eyes. An exit.

With renewed energy, they pushed forward, emerging into a vast cavernous space. The air here was thick with a pungent odor, but they were greeted by the sight of rushing water flowing through a wide channel. The city's sewage system, exactly as Wraith had described.

"This is it," Wraith announced, their voice tinged with relief. "Follow the flow downstream. It should lead to an access grate somewhere on the outskirts of the city."

The journey through the sewage system was a test of their endurance. They waded through knee-deep water, dodging debris and holding their breath as they passed under overflowing pipes. The stench was overpowering, but they pressed on, driven by the desperate need to escape.

Hours bled into one another. Exhaustion gnawed at their limbs, their bodies screaming in protest. Miguel,

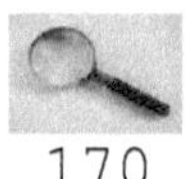

surprisingly, remained the most resilient. The determination to return the Eye of Ra fueled his every step. Finally, after what seemed like an eternity, they spotted a faint glimmer of light filtering through a grate above. Freedom. With a burst of energy, they clambered out of the water, collapsing onto the cold, hard ground gasping for air.

They found themselves in a deserted alleyway, the stench of sewage clinging to their clothes like a second skin. But they were free. Relief washed over them, a bittersweet cocktail mixed with the lingering sting of exhaustion.

"We made it," Snake-Eyes rasped, pulling himself upright. He looked at Miguel, who held the Eye of Ra box protectively. "Good work, kid."

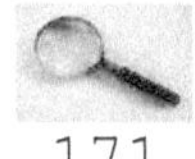

Miguel, a newfound confidence shining in his eyes, offered a shaky smile. "We did it," he echoed.

Suddenly, a voice, cold and calculating, sliced through the night air. "Not quite so fast."

They whirled around to find themselves face-to-face with a lone figure cloaked in darkness. In his hand, a glint of polished metal - a pistol aimed straight at their hearts.

"Crimson Fist," Wraith hissed through their earpiece. "He must have anticipated your escape route."

The revelation sent a jolt of icy fear through Snake-Eyes. Crimson Fist, the notorious black-market auctioneer, stood before them, a predator toying with his cornered prey. The man's face remained shrouded in shadow, but his voice, smooth as polished obsidian, held a hint of amusement.

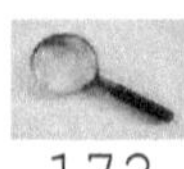

"Well, well, well," he drawled, his gaze sweeping over their disheveled figures. "Look what the sewer system dragged in. It seems escaping my clutches isn't as easy as you anticipated, Snake-Eyes."

Snake-Eyes, ever the strategist, scanned their surroundings. The narrow alley offered little cover, and the only weapon readily available was the rusty pipe Turbo still clutched. He knew a head-on fight wouldn't end well.

"What do you want, Fist?" he rasped, his voice laced with a steely resolve despite the fear gnawing at his gut.

Crimson Fist chuckled, a humorless sound that sent shivers down their spines. "The Eye of Ra, of course. It's the star attraction of tonight's auction, and I wouldn't want it to go missing after all the trouble I went through to acquire it."

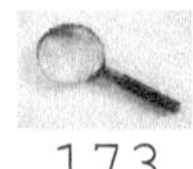

He gestured towards Miguel, who held the box containing the Eye of Ra with a white-knuckled grip. Miguel, though trembling slightly, met Crimson Fist's gaze with defiance.

"You'll never get it," he spat, his voice surprisingly firm.

Crimson Fist's smile vanished, replaced by a flicker of annoyance. He raised his pistol, the click of the chamber sending a fresh wave of terror through the group. "Perhaps you underestimate my resolve, boy," he said, his voice dripping with venom. "But before we resort to unpleasantries, let's see if we can come to an agreement."

Snake-Eyes knew they were in a precarious position. A single bullet could end their mission, and Miguel's life hung in the balance. He needed to buy time, formulate a plan.

"What kind of agreement?" he asked, his voice carefully neutral.

Crimson Fist lowered his pistol slightly, a calculating gleam in his unseen eyes. "You, Snake-Eyes, are a man of many talents. I have a proposition for you. Complete a task for me, and the Eye of Ra, along with your safe passage, is yours."

Snake-Eyes narrowed his eyes. "What kind of task?"

Crimson Fist leaned closer, his voice dropping to a conspiratorial whisper. "There's a shipment arriving at the docks tomorrow night. A shipment containing something very valuable. I want you to steal it for me."

Snake-Eyes' mind raced. Stealing for a notorious criminal wasn't exactly on his moral compass, but it could be their only chance to escape this alive, with the Eye

intact. He glanced at Miguel, a silent question hanging in the air.

Miguel, understanding the gravity of the situation, met his gaze with a determined nod. They had to take the gamble.

Snake-Eyes straightened his shoulders, a steely glint returning to his eyes. "Alright, Fist," he said, his voice firm. "We have a deal."

A slow, predatory smile spread across Crimson Fist's face. "Excellent," he purred. "Consider yourselves… temporarily reprieved. But remember, Snake-Eyes, betrayal comes at a very steep price."

With that, Crimson Fist turned and melted back into the shadows, leaving them alone in the stench-filled alleyway. Relief washed over them, tinged with the bitter aftertaste of their precarious situation.

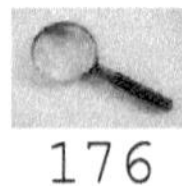

"We're still not out of the woods," Snake-Eyes muttered, his voice laced with a newfound determination. "We need a plan, and fast. Stealing for a criminal isn't ideal, but it might be our only way out."

He looked at Miguel, who stood resolute, the Eye of Ra clutched tightly in his hand. "We'll get you and the Eye back, Miguel. I promise."

Wraith, ever the strategist, chimed in through their earpiece. "I can access Crimson Fist's network and gather intel on this shipment. But stealing it won't be easy. We'll need a flawless plan and some serious firepower."

Snake-Eyes, a flicker of his old fire rekindled in his eyes, nodded curtly. "Then let's get to work."

The night air hung heavy with the promise of another dangerous mission, a desperate gamble for freedom and the fate of an

ancient artifact. As they huddled together in the darkness, a new plan began to take shape, fueled by a thirst for justice and a burning desire to escape the clutches of a ruthless criminal.

Huddled in a safehouse procured by Wraith, Snake-Eyes, Turbo, and Miguel pored over the holographic blueprints of the docks district projected onto a dusty table. The air crackled with a nervous energy as Wraith, their voice disguised by the modulator, outlined the details gleaned from Crimson Fist's network.

"The shipment arrives at Pier 17 tomorrow night," Wraith explained, their holographic finger tracing a route across the shimmering image. "It's guarded by Crimson Fist's mercenaries, a group known for their brutality and trigger-happy tendencies."

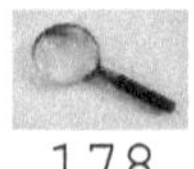

Snake-Eyes, ever the strategist, scowled. "Mercenaries, huh? Sounds like a frontal assault is out of the question."

Turbo, his youthful enthusiasm tempered by the gravity of the situation, chimed in. "So, what's the plan then, Snake-Eyes?"

Snake-Eyes traced a finger along the pier, his eyes narrowing in concentration. "We need a distraction. Something big enough to create a window for us to snatch the shipment and get away clean."

Miguel, surprisingly, spoke up, his voice filled with a newfound resolve. "There's an abandoned warehouse near the docks, filled with old shipping containers. Maybe we can cause a diversion there?"

Snake-Eyes considered the suggestion. "Interesting idea, kid. We could use some kind of explosion to create chaos and draw the guards away from the pier." Wraith, ever the information gatherer, interjected. "There's a power station adjacent to the warehouse. If we can disable it for a short time, it'll cause a blackout, further muddying the waters." A plan, albeit a risky one, began to take shape. Snake-Eyes outlined his vision – a multi-pronged attack that would utilize each of their unique skillsets. Turbo, with his agility and tech skills, would be responsible for disabling the power station. Wraith, their access to Crimson Fist's network proving invaluable, would provide real-time intel and act as their eyes and ears on the ground. Snake-Eyes and Miguel, the muscle of the operation, would infiltrate the docks, using the blackout as cover to steal the shipment and escape. The key, they all knew, was precision and perfect timing.

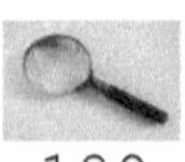

The next day was a blur of activity. Wraith, using their hacking skills, procured coded blueprints of the power station and the docks themselves. Turbo, fueled by nervous energy, tinkered with a makeshift EMP device cobbled together from scavenged parts.

Snake-Eyes, his weathered face etched with grim determination, put Miguel through a series of grueling combat drills. Miguel, surprisingly, proved to be a quick learner, his initial apprehension replaced by a steely focus. He understood the weight of the Eye of Ra and the importance of getting it back to its rightful place.

As dusk settled, casting long shadows across the cityscape, they donned their disguises. Snake-Eyes, a grizzled dockworker with a thick beard and a limp, blended seamlessly into the pre-dawn bustle of the docks. Miguel, disguised as

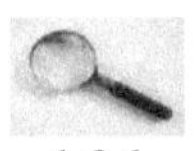

a young delivery boy, followed close behind, his heart pounding a frantic rhythm against his ribs.

Turbo, a nervous knot churning in his stomach, infiltrated the power station, his movements guided by Wraith's murmured instructions through his earpiece. Snake-Eyes and Miguel positioned themselves near Pier 17, the tension thick enough to cut with a knife.

With a silent nod from Wraith, Turbo triggered the EMP device. A surge of energy crackled through the air, followed by an eerie silence. The entire dock district plunged into darkness, the only sound the surprised shouts and curses erupting from the bewildered guards.

This was their cue. Snake-Eyes, his senses on high alert, sprinted towards the designated container, Miguel hot on his heels. The guards, momentarily disoriented by the sudden blackout,

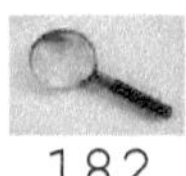

182

scrambled for cover, their shouts echoing through the darkness.

Reaching the container, Snake-Eyes ripped the lock from its hinges with practiced ease. Inside, nestled amongst packing peanuts, was a crate emblazoned with a crimson fist insignia. This had to be it.

Just as they were about to haul the crate away, a guttural roar tore through the night. A hulking figure, presumably a Crimson Fist enforcer alerted by the commotion, charged towards them.

A brutal fight ensued in the heart of the darkened dock. Snake-Eyes, his years of combat experience kicking in, fought with a controlled ferocity, aiming for disarming strikes rather than inflicting serious injury. Miguel, fueled by adrenaline and a newfound sense of purpose, joined the fray, using his agility to his advantage.

The struggle was fierce, the metallic clang of fists against flesh echoing through the empty docks. But with a well-placed kick, Snake-Eyes sent the enforcer sprawling onto the ground, unconscious. Wasting no time, they wrestled the crate out of the container and made a dash for the pre-arranged escape route, a maze of deserted alleys and rusty fire escapes, became their lifeline. Snake-Eyes, with Miguel close behind, navigated the darkness by sheer instinct, his hand gripping the stolen crate tightly. The blackout provided them with a crucial shroud, but they knew Crimson Fist's men wouldn't stay incapacitated for long.

Wraith's voice, a beacon of calm amidst the chaos, crackled through their earpiece. "Power's back up in most sectors. Guards are mobilizing, heading towards your last known location. You need to get out of there, fast!"

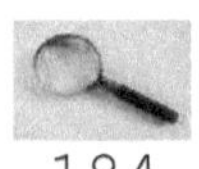

Snake-Eyes cursed under his breath. They were running out of time. Just as they reached a dead end - a towering brick wall blocking their escape, a guttural roar echoed behind them. Flashlights pierced the darkness, illuminating a group of enraged Crimson Fist mercenaries.

"There they are!" one of them bellowed, his voice distorted by rage.

Trapped between a dead end and approaching hostiles, panic threatened to consume Miguel. But Snake-Eyes, ever the strategist, wouldn't let despair cloud his judgment. He scanned the surroundings, his eyes landing on a rickety fire escape clinging precariously to the side of a nearby building.

"Up there!" he barked, shoving the crate into Miguel's arms. "Climb! I'll hold them off!"

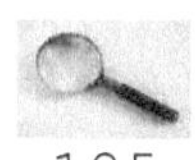

Miguel, understanding the urgency, didn't hesitate. He scrambled onto the fire escape, the metal groaning under his weight. Snake-Eyes, with a silent prayer for the fire escape's integrity, turned to face the approaching mercenaries.

He drew a deep breath, adrenaline coursing through his veins. Years of honed combat skills came to the fore. He fought with the ferocity of a cornered animal, his movements a blur of punches and kicks.

But he was outnumbered and outmatched. A blow landed square on his jaw, sending him reeling. Another sent him sprawling onto the hard concrete floor. Just as a mercenary raised his boot, poised to deliver a finishing blow, a high-pitched whine sliced through the air.

A blur of green and black slammed into the mercenary, sending him flying. It was Wraith, clad in their signature combat

suit, a nightstick held in a white-knuckled grip.

"Go!" Wraith yelled their voice muffled by their mask. "I'll get you some breathing room!"

With a surge of renewed energy, Snake-Eyes scrambled to his feet. He glanced at the fire escape - Miguel was already halfway up, the stolen crate clutched tightly to his chest.

"Almost there, kid!" Snake-Eyes roared, using the last of his strength to shove another charging mercenary aside.

He knew he couldn't hold them off for long. With a final desperate lunge, he grabbed a discarded metal pipe and used it to pry open a rusty dumpster lid. Scrambling inside, he slammed the lid shut just as another blow landed on the spot he'd just occupied.

The world became a muffled cacophony of shouts and metallic clangs as Wraith and

the mercenaries engaged in a fierce battle. Snake-Eyes held his breath, willing the dumpster to hold. Through the thin metal, he could hear the sounds of the struggle fading away.

Finally, after what seemed like an eternity, silence descended. Relief washed over Snake-Eyes, weak and battered but alive. He cautiously poked his head out of the dumpster.

The alleyway was deserted. Wraith, their form silhouetted against the faint moonlight filtering through the smog, stood guard. Miguel, safe and sound, stood on the fire escape, looking down at him with a mixture of relief and concern.

"Come on down," Wraith called out, extending a helping hand.

Snake-Eyes clambered out of the dumpster, his body screaming in protest. He looked at Wraith, a silent question hanging in the air.

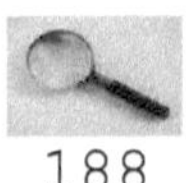

"They're gone," Wraith confirmed. "Seems Crimson Fist decided to cut his losses and retreat for now. But don't think this is over, Snake-Eyes. He won't give up on the Eye of Ra that easily."

Snake-Eyes knew Wraith was right. But for now, they had a brief reprieve. He looked at Miguel, a newfound respect burning in his eyes. The young man had faced danger head-on, proving his courage and determination.

"We got the Eye," Miguel said, his voice trembling slightly, a hint of pride edging through. "Let's get it back where it belongs."

Snake-Eyes nodded grimly. They had a long way to go, but they had taken the first crucial step. With the Eye of Ra secured and a plan forming in their minds, they knew their fight for justice was far from over. The escape from the docks was just

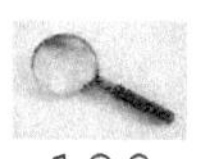

189

the beginning, and the real battle for
the ancient artifact had just begun.
Weeks turned into a blur of planning and
preparation. Their safehouse, a
dilapidated apartment above a noodle shop
in the city's underbelly, became their
base of operations. Wraith, a digital
phantom, scoured the internet for any
information on the Eye of Ra's rightful
home.
Miguel, surprisingly adept with
technology picked up from his time on the
streets, assisted Wraith in deciphering
ancient texts and historical records.
Snake-Eyes, ever the pragmatist, focused
on training Miguel in combat, honing his
reflexes and teaching him self-defense
techniques.
Their shared experience at the docks had
forged a bond between them. Miguel,
initially wary of Snake-Eyes' stoicism,
began to see the unwavering resolve

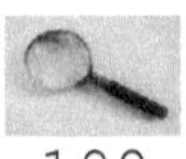

beneath the gruff exterior. Snake-Eyes, in turn, found himself impressed by Miguel's resilience and newfound determination to protect the Eye.

Panic surged through Miguel, his heart hammering a frantic rhythm against his ribs. Snake-Eyes, ever the strategist, remained calm, his mind racing for an escape route. He glanced at Wraith, a silent question hanging in the air.

"Security is on their way, alerted by the disabled cameras," Wraith whispered through their earpiece, their voice laced with urgency. "We're trapped in the vault."

Snake-Eyes knew a head-on fight with Crimson Fist's guards was a losing proposition. He needed a distraction, a way to create an opening. His eyes darted around the high-security vault, landing on a display case containing a collection of ancient throwing weapons.

"Miguel," he hissed, motioning towards the display case. "Get that slingshot." Miguel, understanding Snake-Eyes' plan, scrambled towards the display case, adrenaline masking his fear. As Crimson Fist and his guards advanced, Snake-Eyes grabbed a handful of ceramic shards from a broken urn lying forgotten on the floor.

With a practiced flick of his wrist, Miguel launched a clay ball at the vault's overhead sprinkler system. The fragile clay shattered against the metal, triggering a downpour of water. The guards, caught off guard by the sudden deluge, sputtered in surprise.

Snake-Eyes seized the opportunity. With a cry of defiance, he flung the ceramic shards with deadly accuracy, each shard finding its mark. One connected with a guard's helmet, sending him reeling back with a yell. Another shattered against a

flashlight, plunging the vault into near darkness.

In the ensuing chaos, Snake-Eyes lunged forward. He used the guards' disorientation to his advantage, disarming one with a swift kick and knocking the other unconscious with a well-placed elbow strike to the temple. Crimson Fist, however, remained unfazed. He drew a pistol, its cold metal glinting in the dim light. "This ends now, Snake-Eyes," he snarled, pointing the weapon directly at Miguel.

Wraith reacted with lightning speed. With a blur of movement, they tackled Crimson Fist, sending him sprawling onto the cold, hard floor. The gun clattered across the wet tiles, just out of reach. Snake-Eyes and Miguel didn't hesitate. They knew this wouldn't be enough to stop Crimson Fist for good, but it was their chance. With a final look at the Eye of

Ra, bathed in the soft glow emanating from the box on the pedestal, they bolted towards a hidden service entrance located behind a massive stone statue.

The alarm blared to life, its piercing wail echoing through the museum. Shouts of approaching security guards filled the air. But they were ahead of the chase. The service entrance, a narrow passage normally used for maintenance, offered a desperate escape route.

Squeezing through the narrow passage, they emerged into a deserted back alley. The museum, bathed in the soft glow of floodlights, stood behind them. In the distance, sirens wailed, growing louder with each passing second.

"This way!" Wraith barked, leading them through a maze of back alleys and hidden passageways. Their escape from the museum had been a daring feat, but their ordeal

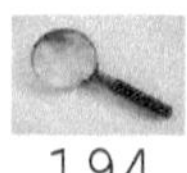

was far from over. Crimson Fist wouldn't give up easily.

They sprinted through the bustling city, adrenaline masking their fatigue. They weaved through crowds, blending in with the throngs of tourists and locals. Miguel, his heart pounding a frantic rhythm against his ribs, clutched the box containing the Eye of Ra close to his chest.

Finally, they reached a pre-arranged rendezvous point – a dilapidated taxi stand on the outskirts of the city. A beat-up old car, its engine idling, awaited them. Their driver, a gruff but reliable smuggler Snake-Eyes had contacted earlier, sat behind the wheel, a knowing glint in his eyes.

With a flurry of activity, they piled into the car. The smuggler, wasting no time, slammed the car into gear and peeled away from the curb, tires

screeching in protest. As the city lights
blurred into streaks of color, they knew
their fight for the Eye of Ra was over.
The stolen artifact, was now safely back
in its rightful place.

The Case of the Missing Mariachi

It was a sweltering summer day in East
Los Angeles, the kind that made the
pavement sizzle and the air feel thick as
molasses. Moe "Snake-Eyes" Juarez, a
grizzled private eye with a reputation
for cracking the toughest cases, sat
behind his desk, fanning himself with a
tattered manila folder.

The door to his office burst open, and in
strode Turbo, Moe's protégé, a wide-eyed
kid fresh off the streets, eager to learn
the ropes of the PI game.

"Jefe, we got a new case," Turbo panted,
wiping the sweat from his brow. "Some big
shot mariachi band leader's gone missing,

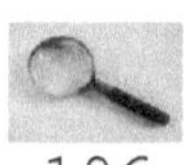

and his wife's offering a fat stack of pesos to find him."

Moe leaned back in his chair, his weathered face betraying no emotion. "Mariachi, eh? Sounds like a tune we better dance to. Grab the keys to the Woody, kid. We're hitting the streets."

They cruised through the barrios of East LA in Moe's trusty 1949 Ford Woody, the rumble of the engine echoing off the sunbaked walls. Turbo kept his eyes peeled, soaking in every detail like a sponge, while Moe navigated the maze of alleys and side streets with the ease of a seasoned pro.

Their first stop was the cantina where the missing mariachi, Julio "El Gallo" Hernandez, had last been seen. The place was a dive, the kind where the tequila flowed like water and the secrets were as thick as the smoke that hung in the air.

Moe flashed his badge at the bartender, a grizzled old-timer with a face like a well-worn saddle. "Talk, amigo, or I'll have the health inspector shut this joint down faster than you can say 'salsa picante.'"

The bartender's eyes widened, and he spilled everything he knew about El Gallo's disappearance, leading them to a seedy motel on the outskirts of town.

As they approached the motel, Turbo's hand hovered near his piece, his knuckles white with anticipation. Moe shot him a warning glance. "Easy, kid. We're here to ask questions, not start a war."

They knocked on the door, and a hulking figure answered, his face twisted into a menacing scowl. Moe flashed his badge again, his voice as smooth as silk. "We're looking for a little bird that flew the coop. You wouldn't happen to

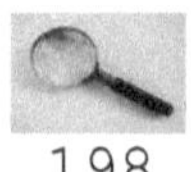

know anything about that, would you, amigo?"

The thug's eyes narrowed, and for a moment, Turbo thought they were in for a rumble. But then, the man's expression softened, and he stepped aside, revealing a battered Julio "El Gallo" Hernandez, tied to a chair and gagged.

Moe and Turbo made short work of the goons, and before long, they had El Gallo safely in the back of the Woody, ready to be reunited with his grateful wife.

As they drove back to the office, Turbo couldn't help but grin. "Jefe, that was some smooth work back there. You really showed me how it's done."

Moe allowed himself a rare smile, his eyes twinkling with pride. "You did good too, kid. Just remember, in this business, it's not about the muscle — it's about the smarts. And you're learning fast."

They pulled up to the office, another case closed, another day in the life of two private eyes working the mean streets of East LA, where the only thing hotter than the sun was the action.

The Rumble at Rios Ranchos

A few days later, Moe and Turbo found themselves embroiled in another case, this one involving a bitter land dispute between two rival ranching families in the outskirts of East LA.

The Rios clan had accused the Ranchos of encroaching on their prime grazing land, and tempers were flaring hotter than a habanero pepper. Moe and Turbo had been hired by the Rios patriarch, Don Esteban, to investigate and hopefully broker a peaceful resolution before things turned ugly.

They pulled up to the Rios Ranch in Moe's trusty Woody, kicking up a cloud of dust

in their wake. Turbo whistled low as they took in the sprawling hacienda, its whitewashed walls gleaming in the afternoon sun.

"Jefe, this place is a palace," Turbo remarked, his eyes wide with wonder.

Moe just grunted, his gaze fixed on the horizon, where the Ranchos' land began. "Don't let the fancy digs fool you, kid. This is cattle country, and out here, a man's worth is measured by the size of his herd and the strength of his resolve."

They were ushered into Don Esteban's study, where the old rancher sat behind a massive oak desk, his weathered face etched with worry.

"Señores, I'm glad you've come," he said, his voice thick with a lifetime of hard living. "The Ranchos have become emboldened, pushing their cattle onto my land, trampling my crops and fouling my

water supply. If this continues, my family will be ruined."

Moe nodded his expression grim. "We'll get to the bottom of this, Don Esteban. You have my word."

Their investigation took them deep into the heart of the disputed territory, where they encountered a group of Ranchos ranch hands, their faces twisted into menacing scowls.

"This is Ranchos land, you hear?" the leader snarled, his hand resting on the butt of his revolver. "You Rios dogs best turn tail and run, before we put you down like the mangy curs you are."

Turbo's hand inched towards his own piece, but Moe stayed his movement with a subtle shake of his head. "Easy, kid. We didn't come here looking for trouble."

But trouble found them anyway, as the Ranchos men drew their guns and opened fire. Moe and Turbo hit the dirt,

returning fire as they scrambled for cover behind a rocky outcropping.

The gunfight raged for what seemed like an eternity, the air thick with the acrid smell of gunsmoke and the whine of ricocheting bullets. Turbo's heart pounded in his chest, his knuckles white as he gripped his revolver, but Moe remained cool and collected, picking off the Ranchos men one by one with surgical precision.

Finally, the last of the Ranchos guns fell silent, and an eerie calm settled over the battlefield. Moe and Turbo emerged from their cover, battered but victorious.

"Jefe, that was some fancy shooting back there," Turbo panted, his eyes wide with admiration.

Moe just shrugged, holstering his weapon. "All in a day's work, kid. Now, let's get

back to the ranch and sort out this mess before more blood gets spilled."

With the evidence they'd gathered and the testimony of the captured Ranchos men, Moe and Turbo were able to broker a truce between the two families, settling the land dispute and restoring peace to the ranching community.

As they drove back to East LA in the Woody, the setting sun painting the sky in brilliant hues of orange and crimson, Turbo couldn't help but feel a sense of pride and accomplishment. He had faced down danger and emerged victorious, all while learning invaluable lessons from his mentor, Moe "Snake-Eyes" Juarez – the toughest, smartest private eye in all of East LA.

The Heist at La Perla Nightclub

A few weeks after the ranch rumble, Moe and Turbo found themselves knee-deep in

another case, this time involving a daring heist at one of East LA's most notorious nightclubs, La Perla.

The owner, a slick operator named Ricky "El Zorro" Delgado, had been robbed of a small fortune in cash and jewels, and he wanted Moe and Turbo on the job to track down the culprits and recover his loot.

They arrived at La Perla just as the sun was setting, the neon sign casting a lurid glow over the rain-slicked streets. Turbo couldn't help but gawk at the joint, his eyes wide with wonder.

"Jefe, this place is something else," he whispered, taking in the sleek lines and art deco styling.

Moe just grunted his expression inscrutable. "Don't let the fancy digs fool you, kid. Places like this are where the real snakes slither."

They were ushered into Delgado's plush office, where the nightclub owner sat

behind a massive mahogany desk, puffing on a thick Cuban cigar.

"Gentlemen, I'm glad you could make it," he drawled, his voice as smooth as silk. "As you know, I've been hit hard, and I need the best in the business to get my goods back."

Moe nodded his steely gaze fixed on Delgado. "We'll get to the bottom of this, amigo. But it'll cost you."

Delgado waved a dismissive hand. "Money is no object, señor. Just get me my stuff back, and you'll be paid handsomely."

Their investigation led them to a seedy part of town, where they tracked down a low-level hood named Chico, who claimed to have information on the heist.

"Alright, Chico, spill it," Moe growled, his fist clenched menacingly. "We know you were in on the job at La Perla, and we want names."

Chico's eyes widened, and he started babbling like a frightened child. "It was Razor Eddie and his crew, I swear! They're holed up in an abandoned warehouse down by the river, divvying up the score."

Moe and Turbo wasted no time, peeling out in the Woody and heading for the warehouse district. As they approached their target, they could see the telltale glow of lanterns flickering through the grimy windows.

"Alright, kid, this is it," Moe whispered, checking the load on his trusty .38. "You ready for some action?"

Turbo nodded his jaw set with determination. "Let's do this, Jefe."

They burst through the doors, guns blazing, catching Razor Eddie and his crew completely off-guard. The ensuing firefight was intense, with bullets

ricocheting off the concrete walls and crates exploding in showers of splinters. Turbo fought like a man possessed, his revolver barking in rapid succession as he cut down Eddie's goons one by one. Moe, ever the cool customer, picked his shots with surgical precision, dropping the crooks with cold efficiency.

Finally, only Razor Eddie remained, cowering behind a stack of crates, his revolver trembling in his hand.

"It's over, Eddie," Moe called out, his voice echoing through the cavernous space. "Drop the gun and come out slow, or you're gonna end up just another chalk outline on the floor."

With a resigned sigh, Eddie emerged, his hands raised in surrender. Moe and Turbo quickly secured him and recovered the stolen loot, a veritable king's ransom in cash and sparkling jewels.

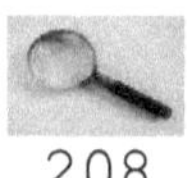

As they loaded Eddie into the back of the Woody, Turbo couldn't help but grin from ear to ear. "Moe, that was some real Hollywood stuff back there. I can't believe we pulled it off!"

Moe allowed himself a rare smile, clapping his protégé on the shoulder. "You did good, kid. Real good. Looks like all that training is paying off."

They returned to La Perla triumphant, Delgado's loot in hand and Razor Eddie trussed up like a Christmas turkey. As they collected their hefty fee, Moe couldn't help but feel a sense of pride in his young partner. Turbo had come a long way from the wide-eyed kid who had first walked through his office door, and Moe knew that with a little more seasoning, the kid just might have what it takes to be a real player in the private eye game.

The Mariachi Masquerade

Just when Moe and Turbo thought they'd seen it all, a new case landed on their doorstep that would test their investigative skills like never before. It started with a frantic knock on the office door, and when Moe opened it, he found himself face-to-face with a distraught young woman named Rosita.

"Señores, you have to help me!" she pleaded, her eyes brimming with tears. "My brother, Manuel, he's gone missing, and I fear the worst."

It turned out that Manuel was the lead singer of one of East LA's hottest mariachi bands, and he had vanished without a trace after their last gig at a high-society party in the ritzy hills overlooking the city.

Moe and Turbo wasted no time, hitting the streets and following the trail of breadcrumbs that Manuel had left behind.

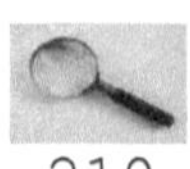

Their investigation led them to a seedy cantina frequented by mariachi musicians, where they learned that Manuel had been involved in a heated argument with a rival bandleader named Ernesto "El Coyote" Ramirez.

"Rumor has it, El Coyote was jealous of Manuel's success," the cantina's bartender whispered, his eyes darting nervously from side to side. "Word on the street is, he had Manuel snatched to teach him a lesson."

Armed with this new lead, Moe and Turbo tracked down El Coyote's hideout, a ramshackle hacienda on the outskirts of town. They approached cautiously, their guns at the ready, but as they neared the compound, they were ambushed by a group of El Coyote's goons.

The ensuing firefight was intense, with bullets whizzing past their heads and the staccato bark of gunfire echoing through

the night. Turbo fought like a man possessed, his revolver barking in rapid succession as he cut down the goons one by one.

Finally, they breached the hacienda's walls and came face-to-face with El Coyote himself, a snarling brute of a man with a face like a clenched fist.

"Looking for someone, cabrones?" he sneered, his hand resting on the butt of his revolver.

Moe's steely gaze fixed on the bandit leader. "We know you've got Manuel, Ernesto. Hand him over, and maybe we'll go easy on you."

El Coyote threw back his head and laughed, a harsh, grating sound that sent chills down Turbo's spine. "Manuel? He's long gone, amigos. But if you want to join him, just keep pushing your luck."

With a flick of his wrist, El Coyote signaled his remaining men, and the

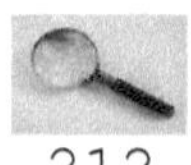

firefight erupted anew. Moe and Turbo took cover behind a crumbling adobe wall, returning fire as best they could.

Just when it seemed like they were outgunned and outmatched, a familiar sound reached their ears - the stirring strains of a mariachi band, growing louder and more insistent with every passing second.

Suddenly, a group of masked mariachi musicians burst through the gates, their instruments blazing like machine guns as they opened fire on El Coyote's men.

Moe and Turbo seized the opportunity, joining the fray with renewed vigor. In the chaos, Turbo caught a glimpse of one of the masked mariachis, and his heart skipped a beat - it was Manuel, alive and well, leading the charge against his captors.

The battle raged on, but in the end, El Coyote's forces were no match for the

combined might of Moe, Turbo, and the
mariachi masquerade. El Coyote himself
was captured, and Manuel was reunited
with his overjoyed sister, Rosita.

As the dust settled and the mariachis
unmasked, Moe couldn't help but shake his
head in disbelief. "Kid, I've seen some
crazy stuff in my time, but this takes
the cake."

Turbo just grinned, his eyes sparkling
with excitement. "Jefe, when you said
this job would be an adventure, you
weren't kidding!"

They returned to their office, battered
but victorious, and as Moe poured them
each a celebratory shot of tequila, he
couldn't help but feel a sense of pride
in his young protégé. Turbo had come a
long way, and Moe knew that with a little
more seasoning, the kid just might have
what it takes to be a real player in the
private eye game - a true East LA legend,

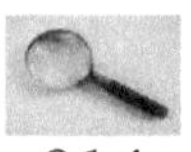

just like his mentor, Moe "Snake-Eyes" Juarez.

The Barrio Bookie Caper

Their next case started with a frantic knock on the office door, and when Moe opened it, he found himself face-to-face with a nervous-looking man named Julio. "Señores, I need your help," Julio pleaded, his eyes darting nervously from side to side. "I've gotten myself mixed up with some bad hombres, and if I don't pay up soon, they're gonna put me six feet under."

It turned out that Julio had been running a small-time bookmaking operation in the barrio, taking bets on everything from cockfights to horse races. But when he got in too deep with a notorious loan shark named Loco Lenny, things took a turn for the worse.

215

"Lenny's goons have been leaning on me hard, jefe," Julio explained, his voice trembling. "They want their money, and they ain't taking no for an answer."

Moe and Turbo wasted no time, hitting the streets and following the trail of breadcrumbs that led them deeper into the seedy underbelly of East LA's gambling scene. Their investigation took them to a dingy pool hall frequented by hustlers and bookies, where they learned that Loco Lenny had been muscling in on all the action, using his crew of enforcers to shake down anyone who didn't pay their vig.

"Lenny's a real piece of work, amigos," the pool hall's grizzled owner whispered, his eyes darting nervously around the smoke-filled room. "He's got half the barrio under his thumb, and anyone who crosses him ends up sleeping with the fishes."

Armed with this new intel, Moe and Turbo tracked down Lenny's hideout, a dilapidated warehouse on the outskirts of town. They approached cautiously, their guns at the ready, but as they neared the compound, they were ambushed by a group of Lenny's goons.

The ensuing firefight was intense, with bullets whizzing past their heads and the staccato bark of gunfire echoing through the night. Turbo fought like a man possessed, his revolver barking in rapid succession as he cut down the goons one by one.

Finally, they breached the warehouse and came face-to-face with Loco Lenny himself, a snarling brute of a man with a face like a clenched fist.

"Well, well, if it ain't the dynamic duo," Lenny sneered, his hand resting on the butt of his revolver. "You boys must have a death wish, coming around here and

sticking your noses where they don't belong."

Moe stepped forward his steely gaze fixed on the loan shark. "We're here for Julio, Lenny. He's paid his debt, and then some. Time to let him go."

Lenny threw back his head and laughed, a harsh, grating sound that sent chills down Turbo's spine. "Paid his debt? That little rat owes me more than he'll ever be able to pay back. But if you're so keen on settling his tab, maybe we can work out a deal."

With a flick of his wrist, Lenny signaled his men, and the firefight erupted anew. Moe and Turbo took cover behind a stack of crates, returning fire as best they could.

Just when it seemed like they were outgunned and outmatched, a familiar voice rang out from the shadows.

"Freeze, cabrones! Drop your guns, or you're all going for a ride downtown!"

It was Julio, flanked by a squad of uniformed police officers, their guns trained on Lenny and his crew.

Lenny's eyes widened in disbelief, but he knew when he was beaten. With a resigned sigh, he dropped his weapon and raised his hands in surrender.

As the cops led Lenny and his goons away in handcuffs, Julio approached Moe and Turbo, a sheepish grin on his face.

"Looks like I owe you boys one, huh?" he said, rubbing the back of his neck. "When Lenny's goons started leaning on me, I knew I had to go to the cops. But I also knew they'd need some muscle to take down Lenny's operation, so I called in the big guns."

Moe allowed himself a rare smile, clapping Julio on the shoulder. "You did good, amigo. Real good. Looks like you've

got more smarts than I gave you credit for."

As they walked out of the warehouse, the first rays of dawn peeking over the horizon, Turbo couldn't help but feel a sense of pride and accomplishment. He had faced down danger once again and emerged victorious, all while learning invaluable lessons from his mentor, Moe "Snake-Eyes" Juarez - the toughest, smartest private eye in all of East LA. And as they climbed into the trusty Woody and headed back to the office, Turbo knew that this was just the beginning of many more adventures to come. With Moe by his side, there was no case too tough, no mystery too complex to solve. East LA was their playground, and they were the kings of the concrete jungle.

The Lowrider Heist

Their next case took Moe and Turbo into the heart of East LA's vibrant lowrider culture. It started with a frantic knock on the office door, and when Moe opened it, he found himself face-to-face with a distraught young man named Chuy.

"Jefe, you gotta help me!" Chuy pleaded, his eyes wide with panic. "My pride and joy, my '49 Chevy, she's been snatched right off the streets!"

For any self-respecting lowrider enthusiast in East LA, having your ride stolen was akin to losing a limb. These meticulously customized cars were more than just modes of transportation - they were works of art, labors of love that represented years of blood, sweat, and tears.

Moe and Turbo wasted no time, hitting the streets and following the trail of breadcrumbs that led them deeper into the

lowrider scene. Their investigation took them to a bustling swap meet, where they learned that a notorious car thief named El Gato had been making a killing by snatching up the baddest lowriders in town and fencing them to the highest bidder.

"El Gato's got a real taste for the finer things, amigos," a grizzled vendor whispered, his eyes darting nervously around the crowded market. "If it's a cherry ride, he'll take it, no questions asked."

Armed with this new info, Moe and Turbo tracked down El Gato's hideout, a secluded chop shop tucked away in a forgotten corner of the barrio. They approached cautiously, their guns at the ready, but as they neared the compound, they were ambushed by a group of El Gato's goons.

Finally, they breached the chop shop and came face-to-face with El Gato himself.

"Well, well, if it ain't the private eyes."

Moe watched the car thief intently. "We're here for Chuy's Chevy, Gato. Hand it over, and maybe we'll go easy on you."

El Gato threw back his head and laughed, a harsh, grating sound that sent chills down Turbo's spine. "That cherry '49? She's long gone, amigos. Sold to the highest bidder, just like all the others."

With a flick of his wrist, El Gato signaled his men.

Just when it seemed like they were outgunned and outmatched, a familiar sound reached their ears - the rumble of powerful engines and the squeal of tires on asphalt.

Suddenly, a convoy of lowriders burst through the gates, their chrome and

candy-apple paint gleaming in the moonlight. Behind the wheel of the lead car was none other than Chuy, his face set in a mask of grim determination.

"Alright, cabrones party's over!" Chuy shouted, revving his engine menacingly. "You're gonna give me back my Chevy, or we're gonna have to do this the hard way."

The lowrider crews swarmed the chop shop, their ranks swelled by reinforcements from every corner of East LA. Moe and Turbo seized the opportunity, joining the fray with renewed vigor.

In the chaos, Turbo caught a glimpse of Chuy's beloved '49 Chevy, its pristine body gleaming like a jewel amidst the clutter of the chop shop. With a burst of speed, he raced towards the car, dodging bullets and flying debris, until finally he reached the driver's side door.

With a triumphant grin, Turbo slid behind the wheel and fired up the engine, the powerful engine roaring to life like a caged beast. He peeled out of the chop shop, Chuy's Chevy leading the charge as the lowrider crews laid waste to El Gato's operation.

In the end, El Gato and his goons were no match for the combined might of Moe, Turbo, and the lowrider legions. El Gato himself was captured, and Chuy was reunited with his beloved Chevy, not a scratch on her gleaming candy-apple paint.

As the dust settled and the lowriders cruised off into the night, Moe couldn't help but shake his head in disbelief.

Turbo just grinned, his eyes sparkling with excitement.

They returned to their office, battered but victorious.

The Sailors Demise

A new case landed on their doorstep that would take them deep into the heart of East LA's simmering racial tensions. It started with a frantic knock on the office door, it was a distraught young man named Lalo.

"Moe, you gotta help me!" Lalo pleaded, his eyes wide with fear. "My little brother, Manny, he's been snatched right off the streets by a bunch of sailors looking for trouble."

It was the summer of 1957, and the city was a powder keg of racial animosity, with tensions between the Mexican-American zoot suiters and the white servicemen stationed in Los Angeles reaching a boiling point. Moe and Turbo knew they were stepping into a minefield, but they couldn't turn their backs on a case like this.

They hit the streets, following the trail of breadcrumbs that led them deeper into the heart of the barrio. Their investigation took them to a seedy pool hall frequented by gang members, where they learned that a group of sailors had been prowling the neighborhood, looking to start trouble with the pachucos.

"It's been brewing for a while," a grizzled old-timer whispered, his eyes darting nervously around the smoke-filled room. "Those sailors, they don't like the way we dress, the way we talk. They think we're a bunch of troublemakers, and they're itching to teach us a lesson."

Armed with this new clue, Moe and Turbo tracked down the sailors' hangout, a rowdy bar near the naval base. They approached cautiously, their guns at the ready, but as they neared the bar, they

were ambushed by a group of drunken sailors spoiling for a fight.

The ensuing brawl was intense, with fists and bottles flying as Moe and Turbo fought their way through the melee. Turbo took a few hard knocks, but he gave as good as he got, his street-honed fighting skills serving him well in the chaos. Finally, they managed to subdue the ringleaders and get some answers out of them. It turned out that Manny had been snatched as part of a twisted initiation ritual, where the sailors would beat up a gang member.

With this new information, Moe and Turbo raced to an abandoned warehouse on the outskirts of town, where they found Manny bound and beaten.

As they untied the young man and helped him to his feet, the sound of approaching footsteps echoed through the cavernous space. Suddenly, they were surrounded by

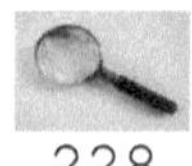

a mob of sailors, their faces twisted into masks of hatred and bloodlust.

"Well, well, if it ain't the dynamic duo," the leader sneered, his fists clenched menacingly. "You boys just couldn't leave well enough alone, could you? Now you're gonna get the same treatment as your little pachuco friend here."

Moe stared at the sailor. "This ends now, amigo. You and your boys are gonna turn around and walk away, or we're gonna have to do this the hard way."

The sailor threw back his head and laughed, a harsh, grating sound that sent chills down Turbo's spine. "You hear that, boys? The greasers think they can take us on!"

With a roar of approval, the sailors surged forward, and the warehouse erupted into chaos. Moe and Turbo fought like demons, their fists and feet a blur of

motion as they cut a path through the
mob.

Just when it seemed like they were
outgunned and outmatched, a familiar
sound reached their ears - the rhythmic
clacking of chains and the defiant cries
of "¡Viva la raza!"

Suddenly, a swarm of gang members burst
through the doors, their faces obscured
by the shadows of their iconic hats and
the drape of their baggy suits. They
descended on the sailors like a pack of
wolves, their chains and fists raining
down blows with savage fury.

Moe and Turbo seized the opportunity,
joining the fray with renewed vigor. In
the chaos, Turbo caught a glimpse of
Manny, his face a mask of determination
as he fought alongside his pachuco
brothers.

The battle raged on, but in the end, the
sailors were no match for the combined

might of Moe, Turbo, and the zoot suit legions. The ringleaders were captured, and Manny was reunited with his overjoyed brother, Lalo.

As the dust settled and the pachucos melted back into the shadows of the barrio."

And as they raised their glasses in a toast to another case closed, Moe couldn't help but feel a sense of hope for the future. Despite the racial tensions that threatened to tear their community apart, there were still those who were willing to stand up and fight for what was right. And as long as there were men like Moe and Turbo on the job, East LA would never be without its champions.

My Other Works Include:
The Robin Hood Virus

The Robin Hood Virus - Discovery

The Robin Hood Virus - Validation

The Robin Hood Virus - Retribution

The Robin Hood Virus - Vindication

Worldwide Trivia from the 1930's including Military Trivia Book 1

Worldwide Trivia from the 1930's including Military Trivia Book 2

Worldwide Trivia from the 1930's including Military Trivia Book 3

A Riverboat Odyssey

A Riverboat Odyssey – Astrid's Final Journey

Moe "Snake Eyes" Juarez – Detective Stories in East Los Angeles during the 1940's

Moe "Snake Eyes" Juarez – Detective Stories in East Los Angeles during the 1950's

Turbo – A Private Detective in East Los Angeles during the 1960's

Turbo – A Private Detective in East Los Angeles during the 1970's

Turbo – A Private Detective in East Los Angeles during the 1980's

234